Mary Lou,
"Happy Birthday!"
2004

THE
GIFT *of*
CHRISTMAS
PRESENT

THE
GIFT *of*
CHRISTMAS
PRESENT

Melody Carlson

Revell

Grand Rapids, Michigan

Published by Fleming H. Revell
a division of Baker Publishing Group
P.O. Box 6287, Grand Rapids, MI 49516-6287
www.revellbooks.com

Second printing, September 2004

Printed in the United States of America

Library of Congress Cataloging-in-Publication Data
Carlson, Melody.
    The gift of Christmas present / Melody Carlson.
        p.   cm.
    ISBN 0-8007-1867-4
    1. Young women—Fiction. 2. Birthparents—Fiction. I. Title.
PS3553.A73257G54 2004
813'.54—dc22   2004004544

Christmas Past: the gift we keep with us forever

Christmas Future: the gift that is yet to come

Christmas Present: the gift we open today

1

Christine studied the tall brick house from the sidewalk. Not unlike the other prestigious homes in this dignified university neighborhood, and yet somehow this one seemed different. She glanced down the tree-lined street to survey the other houses. Obviously, these were old and established residences, not anything like the houses in the neighborhood she'd grown up in, where houses popped up almost overnight, like mushrooms, her father liked to say, and where landscaping was minimal and trees were immature and spindly at best. No, this influential neighborhood appeared well established in both history and wealth. And for some reason that irked her.

But why did this house feel different than the others that lined the street? Was it an aura of heaviness? A feeling of sadness? Or perhaps it was simply the lack of Christmas decorations. No bright evergreen wreath hung on its stark black door. And no cheerful lights helped to relieve the foggy gloom of the late afternoon dusk. She walked up the neat brick walk and rang the doorbell, afraid that to hesitate one more moment might compel her to turn back and abandon this crazy stunt altogether.

After what seemed several minutes, the door slowly opened and the face of an older woman with steely blue eyes and silver hair peered through the slit of the open door.

"Yes?" Her voice had the sound of gravel in it, like someone who had smoked for many years.

"Hello . . . Mrs. Daniels? I'm . . . I'm Christine Bradley—"

"You're late," the woman snapped as she leaned forward on an aluminum crutch to see Christine better. Then she opened the door a little wider to reveal a foot wrapped in elastic bandage. She glared at the girl. "And you may as well know right from the start that I absolutely will not tolerate lateness."

"Late?" Christine said, feeling slightly off balance but curious just the same.

"Yes, the agency said you'd be here an hour ago. And I was just about ready to give up on you completely."

"Oh, I'm terribly sorry." Christine tried her best to smile, deciding to go along with this strange woman's charade, for the moment anyway. At least it delayed the inevitable, which suddenly seemed a good thing, especially since Mrs. Daniels appeared rather abrupt and foreboding, not to mention rude.

"Well, come in here, and close that dang door behind you. I can't afford to heat the entire neighborhood. Despite what some people may think, I have to live within my means."

Christine quickly shut the door, careful not to slam it lest she be chided for that as well. "I'm sorry, Mrs. Daniels, but I have to explain—"

"Look, don't waste my time on apologies or explanations, you're probably not right for the job anyway. Just hang your coat there and then come into the living room and we'll get this over with as quickly as possible." Mrs. Daniels hobbled on her crutches toward a leather club chair, then eased herself down with a loud sigh. "This ankle! I don't know how I could've been so clumsy as to sprain it."

"How did you—"

"Never mind that! I'm the one asking the questions here." She stared openly at Christine as if she were summing her up and finding her lacking. Then she waved her hand as if to dismiss her altogether. "First of all, you're much too young. How old are you, anyway? Sixteen?"

"I'm nineteen, almost twenty."

Mrs. Daniels shook her head. "Well, I wanted an older woman. Someone more responsible. You do understand this is a full-time position, don't you? And it's going to include some evenings as well. I don't want some flighty young thing who thinks she can come and go as she pleases or take off early just because she has a date. I simply won't tolerate it."

You don't tolerate much, Christine thought, but instead she said, "To be honest, I really don't go out much. The Wednesday night worship service, occasionally. But that's about it."

"You're a church girl, then?" Mrs. Daniels's brows lifted with a faint flicker of interest, but her cold blue eyes still looked at Christine as if she could see right through this impromptu deception.

Christine shifted uncomfortably in her chair. What in the world was she doing here? And why on earth had she allowed their conversation to reach this weird place. "Uh, Mrs. Daniels, I need to tell—"

"Just where are your references?" It sounded like an accusation.

"References?" Christine studied this woman's soured expression and decided to continue with the charade.

Mrs. Daniels ran her hand through her short-cropped hair and rolled her eyes in irritation. "Don't they teach you young people anything these days? When you come for a job interview, you're supposed to bring references. I suppose you don't have any. Have you ever held a job before?"

"Actually, I did work at McDonald's during high school, for nearly two years."

Mrs. Daniels laughed but with no mirth. "Now, that's real handy. Maybe you could go into the kitchen there and whip me up a Big Mac for dinner. Good grief, girl, do you know anything about housekeeping?"

"Housekeeping?"

"Oh, I don't know why I'm even bothering with you, Miss . . . Miss—what was your name again?"

"Christine. Christine Bradley."

"Right." Her eyes narrowed. "Well, Miss Bradley, tell me, do you even know the difference between a mop and a broom?"

Christine nodded slowly. "I did keep house for my father during the last six years." A lump grew in her throat as she suddenly realized how much she missed him as well as the familiarity of her previous home.

Mrs. Daniels looked skeptical. "And what did your mother do?"

"My mother died," Christine said quietly. *Twice*, she thought.

"Oh, well, that's too bad." Mrs. Daniels seemed to soften just a little. "But at least it seems you do know how to keep house, then?"

Christine nodded again, ready to end this ludicrous interview, but not quite ready to divulge her true identity to this antagonistic woman. How could someone this cold, this calculating, actually be her genetic grandmother? Perhaps she'd made a mistake somewhere, gotten it all wrong. But she knew that was impossible. Without a doubt this must be the right woman. It was the right address, the right town, the right name. But just the same it was all wrong. Terribly wrong!

"Mrs. Daniels," Christine began again. "I really need to—"

"Well, I really need you to write down those references for me, and if they meet my satisfaction, and if no one better shows up, well, then you can start work right away. My daughter-in-law is wearing on my nerves these days. And she said just today that she can't keep this up forever, especially during the holidays, which is perfectly fine by me. The less I see of that woman, the happier I'll be. For the life of me, I still can't see why my stepson ever married someone like her to begin with."

That must be my uncle, Christine thought. Although her father had never mentioned anything about Lenore's other

11

siblings. But then maybe he was a stepuncle. She wasn't sure. And her father hadn't really known much about her birth family in the first place, other than the name and the town, and that had been discovered only recently and quite by coincidence.

"And those grandkids aren't anything to brag about either. A couple of spoiled brats, if you ask me, always whining and complaining and getting underfoot."

"But how fortunate you are to have family that—"

"Fortunate?" Mrs. Daniels scowled. "Why, they're just waiting for me to croak so they can inherit all this." She waved her hand around, then laughed in a sharp, cynical way. "But what they don't know won't hurt them. And, just so you'll know, Miss Bradley, just in case you're thinking you can sneak in here and steal from the old broad, well, you'd better think again. I may be pushing eighty, but I've still got all my marbles up here." She pointed to her head. "Not that my family thinks so. I'm sure they'd love to declare me senile and have me committed to some old folks home to whither away and die." She leaned forward and peered at Christine. "Felicity didn't send you here, did she?"

"Felicity?" Christine said, feeling more and more like she'd just stepped into the twilight zone.

"My daughter-in-law," Mrs. Daniels said with a frown. "That girl is out to get me. I just know it."

"But why?" Despite her reservations and a longing to escape this cantankerous woman, Christine felt herself being reeled in. She sensed there was a reason that Mrs. Daniels was so bitter and jaded. And she wanted to know what it was.

"Like I said, they're after my money." She got a sly smile, as if she were keeping a secret. "And that's perfectly fine with me. I plan to keep stringing them along just to ensure that they show me a bit of respect during my final years. I'm sure that's the only reason they even attempt to be nice to me—thinking I'm going to leave my *vast* fortune to them." She laughed again, only this time the hollow sound seemed to echo with sadness as it reverberated through the impeccably decorated rooms of the large, quiet house.

Inexplicably, and to her own irritation, Christine felt a real wave of pity for this embittered woman. And although it seemed impossible to think they were actual blood relatives, she felt some strange kind of connection.

"Okay, Mrs. Daniels, I'll write down my references for you. I can give you my pastor's name and number, and my manager at McDonald's. I could give you my father's phone number too, but he recently left the country to teach at a mission base down in Brazil. Will just two names be enough?"

"I guess it'll have to do. But mark my word, young lady, in the future if you should ever apply for a job again, you had better bring your references along with you!" With a loud groan, she pulled herself to her feet and then struggled for her crutches. "Young people nowadays!"

Christine stood too. "So when do you want me to come?"

"Well, Felicity is coming back today. Why don't you come tomorrow at eight o'clock sharp, but not a minute before since I don't get up until eight. And if you can promise to come tomorrow, I can tell Felicity that she no longer needs to bother herself with me. Actually, I've been telling them both that since I got home from the emergency room last Saturday, but do they listen to me? Ha! Not on your life." The woman arranged her crutches beneath her arms, then hobbled away without even saying good-bye or seeing Christine to the door.

Christine pulled a small notebook out of her purse, neatly wrote down the references, and left them on the gleaming mahogany table in the foyer. Then quietly she slipped on her parka and let herself out the front door. It was already getting dark outside, and she shivered against the cooling temperature. She hurried down the walk and questioned what she was getting herself into. But then again she had wondered what she'd do with herself during Christmas break. Surely this would be a holiday she'd never forget.

2

"You're sure you'll be okay on your own during the holidays?" Christine's roommate asked as she shoved her dirty clothes into a laundry sack. "We've got a full house, but you're welcome to come home with me if you don't mind sleeping on the floor."

Christine picked up a dirty sock and tossed it into Brianna's rapidly filling bag. "Thanks anyway, but I've taken a job during the holidays."

"You're going to work during Christmas?"

She nodded. "It should be pretty interesting too."

Brianna frowned as she attempted to tie the bulging bag closed. "Sounds like a drag to me. But then I've never found work to be terribly engaging."

Christine didn't say anything, but she knew firsthand this was true. She'd only just met Brianna at the beginning of fall term, when they'd been paired off to share a room, but in the past few months she'd witnessed up close and personal how this less-than-motivated girl allowed her side of the room to pile up until she practically needed a snow shovel to unearth her bed.

"Well, you have fun now," Brianna said with a bright smile.

"Thanks," Christine said, although *fun* hardly seemed the appropriate word to describe her new housekeeping job for the demanding Mrs. Daniels. "And you have a good Christmas with your family," she called as Brianna struggled to get out the door, loaded down with her backpack and laundry bag.

Christine lingered in the unusually quiet hallway for a few moments. It was amazing how quickly the place had evacuated following finals. She wouldn't be surprised if she was the only one left on this floor by now. Finally she went back into her room, closed the door, and locked it. She glanced around the small space and told herself that she should appreciate these next few weeks of peace and quiet. And yet somehow she knew it wouldn't be quite that simple.

She sat down at her desk and reopened her father's latest letter. He was writing only weekly now, if that. When he'd first arrived down there, she'd gotten letters from him almost every other day. She thumbed through the recent photos he'd sent. His tanned face looked years younger and more relaxed than it had in ages. In fact, he hardly appeared to be sixty-four. She felt certain this must be the result of his new teaching position down at the mission in Brazil.

"It's always been a lifetime dream of mine," he'd confessed to her last year. "Long ago, back when I was still in college, back before I met your mother, I seriously considered becoming a foreign missionary. For some reason I fancied the idea of South America. I suppose it was because of all those missionary books I'd been reading. But I'd sent for the mission information and had even begun filling out an application."

"And then you met Mom and decided to get married instead?" Christine had asked.

"It didn't seem like such a difficult decision at the time. Once I met your mother, I knew she was all I'd ever wanted. It felt as if she brought everything I'd ever missed into my world." He'd smiled. "And she made my life seem more alive and happy and full."

"You were really in love, weren't you."

Christine had always enjoyed hearing her dad talk about their romance—how he had just been starting out in his teaching profession and her mother had been a registered nurse, how they'd met at church and fallen in love almost instantly. It was straight out of a storybook. And she still hoped that someday she'd have a similar experience herself. Although so far it didn't seem terribly likely.

"I was so completely smitten," he'd confessed last year, "that I forgot all about wanting to be a foreign missionary. I was just happy to have a good job at the local elementary school, to marry your sweet little mother, and to live happily ever after."

"But are you happy now?" she'd asked. "In your work, I mean."

He'd frowned slightly. "Oh, I don't know . . ."

"Then why don't you do it?" she'd said suddenly. "Why don't you just go for it, Dad? Revive your old dream and just do it. I mean, lots of people your age take off to do something different. And you've been saying you're going to take early retirement ever since Mom died, but you keep putting it off."

"I just wanted to make sure you were settled," he'd said. "I wanted to be here for you during your first years of college."

"And you've done that, Dad. But you know I'll be transferring to the university for my junior year. I won't even be living at home after next summer." She'd looked around the familiar kitchen, memorizing the cheerful yellow and white checked wallpaper her mother had hung back when Christine was still in grade school. "You know, Dad, you could even sell the house if you wanted. I mean, I'd totally understand."

"Oh, no, no." He'd waved his hand. "I wouldn't do that, Christine. Where would you come home to during your vacation times?"

But, as it turned out, he'd leased the house, for just two years, but there'd also been talk of signing an option to buy, although Christine wasn't sure about that. Still, it had seemed the sensible thing to do at the time, what with her off at college and him planning to be out of the country. And Christine had assured him that she would be perfectly fine on her own. She'd had a part-time job, a partial scholarship, and faith that God would see her through. So far so good.

She stared at the recent photos of her father amidst the smiling brown faces of schoolchildren until her eyes became too blurry to focus and she feared that her tears would ruin the pictures completely. "Oh, how I miss you,

Daddy," she said as she carefully stacked the pictures and placed them back in the envelope.

Of course, she knew he wasn't her "real" father. Or, more accurately, her biological father. And she knew the only mother she'd ever known wasn't her birth mother. But they'd both been her *real* parents, and she'd loved them as much, perhaps even more, than if they'd shared the same gene pool. And now that she was completely alone and on her own, she missed them both more than ever.

She picked up the family portrait on her desk. It had been taken just about a year before her mother had suffered the brain aneurysm that had so unexpectedly taken her life. Christine remembered the day as if it were yesterday. She'd just started her freshman year in high school. It had been the first week and her mother had dropped her off at the front entrance.

"Have a good day, honey," she'd said, just like always. Then she'd added rather unexpectedly, "And don't forget that God's always watching out for you."

Christine had nodded, then uttered a quick good-bye before she dashed from the car. It wasn't that she was embarrassed, exactly, to be seen emerging from a seventeen-year-old peach-colored sedan with a dented front fender, or even to be seen with a slightly frumpy mother who was quite a bit older than most of her friends' parents, but the truth was she wasn't eager to be seen like that either. And certainly not during the first week of school, especially when she'd been trying extra hard to make a good impression. At the time it had seemed incredibly important to look cool, and Christine's parents, home, and car didn't fall anywhere close to the cool category. But then life and values can change in a heartbeat. And by the end of that day, Christine couldn't have cared less about appearances. All she wanted was her mother back. But that wasn't going to happen.

She and her father had grieved together, helping each other along like the blind leading the blind. Her first year of high school passed almost without notice. But eventually their lives fell into something of a pattern. Something that vaguely resembled normal. Not that it was anything like when her mother was alive. But they got by. And Christine slowly learned a bit about housekeeping and grocery shopping and how to do laundry without turning her father's jockey shorts pink. She had never fully realized or even appreciated all that her stay-at-home mother had done to make their lives pleasant and comfortable and easy.

It was midway through this year of grieving and getting by that her father had broken the news to her. As life turned out, Christine had lost not just one mother but two.

"Your mother wanted to tell you several years ago," he'd said one evening in late winter. "But I thought it was unimportant. I thought we were all the parents you'd ever need, the only ones you've ever known. But now that Marie is gone, well, I think maybe it's time you knew the truth."

"The truth?" Christine had felt as if her world was suddenly shifting again. She'd felt the need to grab on to something before she went totally sideways.

"This isn't easy for me, honey. I've always thought of you as our very own. And, believe me, you are. But not completely." He'd paused to take a deep breath. "The fact of the matter is we adopted you at birth."

Christine had blinked. How could this be? "I'm adopted?"

He'd nodded. "Marie and I had always wanted to have children, but the good Lord just never saw fit to give us any—until you, that is. You were our little miracle child."

Christine had tried to take in his story, but at the time she'd been in such a state of shock that much of it went right past her. She'd had him retell the story days later, more slowly and carefully, so that she could begin to put the pieces together in her own mind. Her birth mother was Lenore Blackstone, an eighteen-year-old who had left home because of an unwanted pregnancy.

"Lenore's parents were unsympathetic," her father had explained. "Her condition was an embarrassment to them. So Lenore moved from her hometown to Larchwood and got a job at Buddy's Café. Marie and I were regulars there and knew all the waitresses by name. So, naturally, we noticed whenever a new girl came along. We quickly befriended Lenore and learned that she was on her own and lonely and frightened. She was renting a room above the hardware store but was barely able to make ends meet. When Marie learned that Lenore was pregnant, she invited her to come to church with us, and eventually we offered her a room in our home. We both loved Lenore and felt right off the bat that she was like family. As the end of her pregnancy drew near, she began to suggest that we might want to adopt her baby. We were a bit stunned at first, but the more we thought about it, the more it seemed to make sense. Most of all, Lenore wanted to ensure that her baby had a good home."

Christine had patted her father's hand. "And you and Mom saw to that."

He'd nodded. "We did our best. Your mom even gave up her job as a nurse just so she could be a full-time mother to you. We didn't mind the extra scrimping, not one bit. You were worth it."

"But what happened to my birth mother?"

"It was only about a month after you were born. We could both see that Lenore was an intelligent girl, and we encouraged her to register for classes at the community college. We even offered to pay her tuition, since she had no intention of going back to her family just then. It was a freezing day in January, and she'd just gotten off the bus near campus, when she was struck down by a car that had skidded across the icy pavement. She went into a coma and died two days later."

Christine had felt her eyes filling with tears for a woman she'd never even really known.

"Marie and I were just devastated." Her dad had sadly shaken his head. "We made arrangements for her funeral and desperately tried to locate her family in the town she'd said she'd come from, but there wasn't a single Blackstone listed in the phone book. That's when Marie wondered if perhaps Lenore had made up the name to distance herself from her family."

"Maybe she didn't want to be found," Christine had suggested.

But, as it turned out, Lenore hadn't made up the name at all. Only last summer while getting his traveling shots at the county health department, Christine's dad had met a man named Blackstone, and out of curiosity he'd inquired further. The man told him about a second cousin, Allen Blackstone, who had lived in the same town Lenore had come from and who had also had a daughter by that name. Unfortunately, Allen had died of a heart attack when Lenore was still a young teenager, and her mother had remarried only a year or so later. The man wasn't absolutely certain, but he thought the second husband's name was Daniels and that he was some bigwig at the university.

"Isn't it ironic," her father had said as they sat at the kitchen table, eating the chicken casserole she'd prepared that afternoon, "that you're already enrolled to go to college in that very same town. It's possible that you could have a grandmother there."

"I don't care if I do," Christine had said as she refilled her water glass.

Her father's brows had raised slightly. "Wouldn't you like to meet her?"

"Not if she was that horrible to my birth mother. Really, Dad, why would I want to have anything to do with someone like that?"

"I don't know . . ." Her father had taken another bite and then smiled. "Good dinner tonight, Christine. Your mother would be proud."

Which mother? Christine had wondered. But, of course, she knew who he meant. Naturally, he could only be speaking of Marie, the only mother Christine had ever known. Still, it bothered her that she'd begun to wonder about this other mother, the one who had died at an even younger age than Christine was now. What was Lenore Blackstone really like, anyway? And what was wrong with her family that they would abandon her like that?

Well, starting tomorrow, Christine would find out. The big question was, Would she spill the beans to her biological grandmother? Or would she simply play along in the housekeeper role and discover these things for herself? She wondered what her father would recommend, but, of course, she knew. He would be quick to quote something like "Honesty is the best policy." And under normal circumstances she would agree with him completely. But this was anything but normal.

3

Esther Daniels cursed as she attempted to shove herself up from the low-seated chair where she'd fallen asleep in the living room. She wondered why she bothered to put up with these blasted wingback chairs anymore. It wasn't as if they were comfortable. And at her age she should be sitting in a recliner, maybe even one with vibrating massage or a heater or one of those lift-seat contraptions she'd seen on television commercials. Oh, sure, they were ugly as sin, but they did the trick, didn't they? Who cared about looks at her age? She looked around her impeccably decorated living room and rolled her eyes. "Hang those decorators, anyway!" she muttered as she finally managed to prop her crutches beneath her arms and steady herself. "What do they know about comfort?"

She'd been speaking to herself more and more as the years passed. At first she'd questioned this odd behavior a bit, but after a while she'd decided it was better than the lonely silence that always prevailed in the large, empty

25

house. Besides, what did she care if some people thought she was batty? Let them live all by themselves in a big old house and see how they liked it. Oh, she'd considered selling her home several times, but at the last moment she'd always reneged. Perhaps it was a matter of pride, or maybe it was just plain old laziness, but Esther had decided to remain here until her last days. They'd have to carry her out feet first.

"What about checking out some of those nice retirement homes?" Jimmy had suggested to her just recently.

"You're not putting me in some old folks home," she'd told him. "Not as long as I'm able to walk and talk and breathe."

Of course, it wasn't long after she'd spoken those words that she'd slipped on her patio and sprained her right ankle. But even if she couldn't walk, she could still talk and breathe, and she had absolutely no intention of being locked up in one of those smelly old folks homes like she'd taken her own mother to live in. Of course, her mother had been without funds at the time and her choices limited. Esther had told herself that she was doing the poor old woman a favor. Now she wasn't too sure. But there was no going back. Only forward. And the prospects of that weren't terribly encouraging.

"Growing old is for the birds," she said as she opened her large double-wide refrigerator and peered in. "Orange juice, one-percent milk, Fuji apples, cottage cheese . . ." She rattled off the contents as if she were reading a menu, then picked up the cottage cheese carton and shook her head. That obtuse Felicity! Wouldn't she know by now to get the low-fat kind? Was she trying to give her mother-in-law a heart attack? Esther put the carton back into the refrigerator and slammed the door. "Maybe I'm not hungry after all."

Just then the phone rang, causing her to jump. "Who could that be?" she grumbled as she hobbled over to answer the wall phone next to the granite-covered breakfast bar.

"Hello?" she said, more of a growl than a greeting.

"Mom?"

"Hello, Jimmy. Did you know that harebrained wife of yours got me the wrong kind of cottage cheese again? I think she's just doing this to spite me. I have half a mind to—"

"Oh, that's probably my fault," Jimmy said. "I don't like the low-fat kind myself, and she probably got confused."

"Well." Not for the first time she wondered why he was protecting that woman. Furthermore, she wondered what exactly it was about that woman that had attracted him in the first place. Esther had always considered her stepson to be a fairly sensible young man. Well, until he'd gone and married that flibbertigibbet. Oh, she wasn't blind; she could admit that Felicity was beautiful and could occasionally even be charming. But most of the time Esther thought the young woman's head was just stuffed with fluff.

"I wanted to check and see how you were doing, Mom," Jimmy said. "Can we get you anything? Felicity and I got a sitter and are going to a Christmas party tonight, but we could stop by and bring you something first."

"I don't need anything," she said sharply. "Well, other than some low-fat cottage cheese, that is."

"We'll drop some by."

"Oh, don't bother." She sighed. "Don't go to the trouble."

"It's no trouble, Mom. The party is near your house anyway."

"Whose party is it?" Suddenly she felt interested. She remembered the days when she'd been invited to the best university parties. Back when James was alive.

"It's at the Stanleys'," Jimmy said.

"Oh," Esther said in a flat voice. "Well, they aren't so terribly smart. Don't even know how they can afford a home over here in the first place."

"They're nice people, Mom."

"So say you."

She heard him sigh over the phone and knew that was the signal that his patience was wearing thin. Well, what did it matter to her? Her patience was worn thin too. And, besides that, he was the one who had called her.

"Anything else you need?"

"No," she snapped. "As a matter of fact, I don't need anything. Don't bother yourselves to stop by—"

"It's no bother, Mom."

"No, no . . . ," she said, regretting that she was using such a sharp tone on Jimmy. Sometimes she wondered what made her so cranky and mean. "Don't bother yourselves with me, Jimmy. I'll have my girl go out and get me whatever I need tomorrow."

"Your girl?"

"Yes. I've hired a housekeeper."

"A housekeeper? Are you sure about this?"

"Of course I'm sure. Good grief, Jimmy, do you think I'm going senile on you? Or getting Alzheimer's? Or just plain decrepit and helpless? I've hired a girl, and I will be perfectly fine. Please tell Felicity there's no need for her to stop by anymore."

"Are you sure?"

"Jimmy!"

"Okay. Fine, Mom. Just let us know if you need anything, will you?"

"If I need anything, I'll have my girl go get it for me."

"All right. Then have a good evening, Mom."

She laughed in her customary way. It was her way of showing that someone had said something completely ludicrous. "Oh, sure, Jimmy. I'll have a wonderful evening. Thank you so very much!" Then she hung up the phone with a loud bang.

Oh, she knew she was a mean old crow, and sometimes she even regretted it. But she'd spent most of her life acting gracious and courteous and nice—the way the wife of an important man should act. But things had changed. She was old and alone now. Why continue the act? Besides, she told herself as she hobbled back to the refrigerator, if a person couldn't get ornery when she was old, what was the use of getting on in years?

She stood before the open refrigerator, peering in to see the exact same contents as before. Finally she took an apple, stuck it into the pocket of her oversize sweater, and tottered off toward her bedroom, turning off the lights as she went. No sense wasting electricity. She was careful not to catch her crutch on edges of the Oriental rug that ran down the length of the hardwood floor. Another fall could be her undoing.

She turned on the bedroom light to reveal tall walls of

pale blue and ivory. The striped wallpaper had an elegant moiré pattern that had been popular during the eighties. Along the walls stood a few pieces of gleaming cherry furniture, all very expensive and all in the Queen Anne style, including her king-size four-poster bed. It was centered between two tall windows, and beneath it was a large Persian rug in shades of blue and ivory. Some might think the room overly formal and cool, but it suited Esther. Or so she liked to tell herself. She occasionally considered changing the ivory satin bedspread to something a little softer and cozier, but somehow she never got around to it.

She removed the apple from her pocket and set it on the bedside table, then struggled to balance herself on one foot as she attempted to remove her clothing without toppling over. Finally she gave up and climbed into bed still half dressed. She turned off the light and waited in the darkness for sleep to come and rescue her. Sleep and dreams seemed her only respite from this ongoing endurance race called life. Sometimes, especially lately, she wondered why she even bothered to participate at all. What was there to live for, anyway? Her doctor had prescribed some powerful pain pills when she'd sprained her ankle, but she'd taken only a couple, and those on the first day. She thought the rest might come in handy some other day. She just wasn't sure which day that would be. She considered taking one now, but at the moment she was simply too exhausted to climb out of bed and get them. Like so many other things in her life, it would have to wait.

4

Christine pushed the doorbell again. It was ten minutes after eight, and, as she recalled, Mrs. Daniels (she couldn't bring herself to call her Grandmother, not even in her mind) had said not to arrive before eight. She hadn't specified exactly when to come, or maybe Christine had been too flustered to listen correctly. But 8:10 seemed a safe time to show up for her "job." During her twenty-minute walk across campus, on her way to Mrs. Daniels's home, she had attempted to convince herself that was all this was. A job. Suddenly she wasn't so sure.

The door opened a crack. "Who is it?" demanded a voice that sounded like Mrs. Daniels's, only huskier than before.

Christine peered through the two-inch crack. "It's me, Christine Bradley," she said. "Your . . . your housekeeper."

The door opened wide enough to show that Mrs. Daniels had a pale blue bathrobe draped over her.

"I'm sorry," Christine said. "Did I get you up?"

"No." Mrs. Daniels stepped back and waved her inside. "Get in here before my house gets cold."

Christine stepped inside and quickly closed the door behind her. She stared at the frazzled old woman, unsure if this was actually the same Mrs. Daniels she'd met yesterday. Her short silver hair was sticking out in every direction, and she had on some wrinkled tan slacks with a pink pajama top beneath the robe that appeared to be half on and half off.

"Well, don't just stand there gaping at me," Mrs. Daniels snapped. "I know I look a fright. I didn't sleep well last night, and I need some help getting dressed right now. You are able to do that, aren't you?"

"Of course."

"Then follow me."

Christine followed the old woman down the long hallway. In the dim light she could see that several works of art hung on the walls. Even her inexperienced eye could tell they were originals and probably valuable. She would've liked to have taken time to examine them more closely, but Mrs. Daniels had already made it to the room at the end of the hall.

"Come on, come on," the old woman called. "Don't dawdle."

Christine hurried along and followed her into a very elegant bedroom suite. The room was about twice the size of the living room Christine had grown up with and was decorated like something out of a magazine. Other than the unmade bed, only one side actually, and a few articles of clothing on the floor, everything was absolute perfection.

"This is a beautiful room," Christine said as she watched Mrs. Daniels easing herself into a pale blue velvet chair by the window.

"Yes, yes." Mrs. Daniels frowned. "I hope never to catch you snooping around in my things, Miss . . . Miss . . . What is your name again?"

"Christine." She tried to smile. "Christine Bradley."

"Yes, that's right." She nodded. "Miss Bradley. Anyway, I won't put up with any snooping . . . or stealing either, for that matter." She peered up at Christine. "You say you're a churchgoing girl, right?"

"That's right."

"Well, I expect that means you should be honest. At least that's what it used to mean. Not too sure what it means anymore. But I will not put up with any shenanigans, you understand?"

Christine swallowed and nodded, still incredulous that this woman was a flesh and blood relative. She studied the old woman's long, straight nose and wondered if it didn't look a bit like her own. Or perhaps she was imagining things.

"Fine. Now help me get these ridiculous trousers off. I don't know what got into my crazy daughter-in-law's head yesterday, helping me put these confounded things on. I told her I should stick to loose, stretchy garments until my ankle heals up. But, oh no, she thought I should dress up nicely. She's a ridiculous young woman!"

Christine felt a bit embarrassed as she helped the old woman slip out of the lined wool trousers, carefully slipping the narrow pant leg past the oversize, bandaged foot. She couldn't help but notice the pale, scrawny legs. *How awful to grow old,* she thought as she turned away and laid the trousers on the bed.

"Don't leave those pants on the bed," the woman chided as she pulled the bathrobe around her. "There." She pointed to the wall with two doors. "The closet is on the right. Find a pants hanger and hang them up. Then find me a jogging suit." She cackled. "Not that I plan to do any jogging. Get the blue velour one, please. Those pants have extra-wide legs as I recall."

Christine walked into the large closet. It was about the size of her dorm room, only completely outfitted with shelves and drawers and rods full of beautiful clothes. Expensive clothes. And shoes! She'd never seen so many shoes—that weren't in a store, anyway. She quickly located what appeared to be the more casual section of the closet and found not one but two blue velour jogging suits.

"Do you mean the dark blue or the light blue?" she called from the closet.

"The darker one, I think."

Christine emerged with a jogging suit. "This one?"

"Yes, that's it. I don't care much for that color on me, but at least it will be comfortable." Mrs. Daniels was attempting to stand now, struggling to get the crutches in place. "However, I've decided I want to take a shower after all. I'll need you to help me with the bandage."

So Christine followed her into a large bathroom where everything was white. White marble tiles, white fixtures, and white towels. Mrs. Daniels lowered herself onto a metal bench topped with a white velvet cushion. She stuck out her bad foot and groaned slightly. "Be careful when you unwrap it," she warned. "It's still very tender."

Christine knelt down and gently untwined the layers of elastic bandage until she exposed a very swollen and odd-colored foot. It was shades of yellow, purple, and black. "Oh, my," she said as she laid the bandage on the counter. "That looks like it hurts."

"Of course it hurts," Mrs. Daniels snapped, her brows drawn tightly together.

"I'm sorry."

"Well, it's not your fault." Mrs. Daniels seemed to soften just a bit. "And I suppose the pain is making me a little grouchier than usual."

Christine took some comfort in the old woman's confession. "That's understandable."

"Besides that, I'm old," Mrs. Daniels said. "I've earned the right to be a curmudgeon if I feel like."

Christine smiled. "That's not a word you hear every day."

"Well, I used to teach English. Back in the days when students were expected to have an actual vocabulary."

Christine stood, feeling a bit overwhelmed at the idea of helping this old woman bathe. How on earth had she gotten herself into this crazy mess, anyway? "Do you want me to start the water in the shower for you?"

"Yes."

So Christine turned on the water and adjusted it to what felt like the right temperature, then stepped back. "That's nice that you've got a place to sit down in there," she said. "That should make it easier for you."

"That's the whole point," Mrs. Daniels said. "Now turn your back while I get into the shower, but don't leave.

I may need your help getting out. I haven't actually attempted this yet."

"All right." Christine waited until she heard the shower door close. Then she picked up the bathrobe and pajama top and wondered what to do next. She decided to move the bench close to the shower for when Mrs. Daniels got out. She also set a couple of thick white towels on the edge of it. Next, she located a thick white bath mat, which she placed right next to the shower entrance.

"Okay, I'm done now," Mrs. Daniels called from inside the shower stall. "Hand me a towel."

Much to her relief, Christine managed to open the shower door and hand the old woman a towel without seeing too much old, wrinkly flesh.

"Now give me a hand," Mrs. Daniels said. She was wrapped in the towel and struggling to balance on one foot. "And hurry it up, my ankle is starting to throb."

Christine prayed as she helped the old woman out of the shower and eased her onto the bench, amazingly without a mishap.

Mrs. Daniels groaned. "Maybe I should've skipped the shower after all."

Christine got a smaller towel, and without asking she began to blot the dripping silver hair. Fortunately, Mrs. Daniels didn't protest.

"Let's get you dried and bandaged up again," Christine said with a bit more authority. She wrapped another towel around Mrs. Daniels's shoulders before she stooped down to help dry her legs and feet. Then, kneeling on the hard marble floor, she carefully rewrapped the ankle as closely as she could to the way it had been before she'd unwound it.

"Have you done this before?"

She shook her head. "No, but I had considered going to nursing school for a while."

"Whatever for?"

"To become a nurse." Christine stood.

"Well, of course. But why on earth would anyone want to become a nurse, of all things? Changing bedpans and caring for sick people. Good grief."

"As it turned out, I wasn't really suited for it." Christine handed her a white terry bathrobe that was hanging on a hook by the shower.

"You could've fooled me." Mrs. Daniels pushed the bathrobe back at her. "No, just go and get me my clothes. I believe I'll just get dressed in here. You'll find my underthings in one of the top drawers in the closet. And while you're at it, bring me a sturdy tennis shoe for my good foot."

After about twenty minutes and a bit of cursing on Mrs. Daniels's part, they managed to get her adequately dressed and seated on the pale yellow leather couch in the living room.

"I think you should put your foot up," Christine advised.

"Yes, I'm sure you're right."

"And I think you should have some breakfast." Christine adjusted the tapestry pillow beneath the injured foot. "What do you usually have?"

"I'll start with some orange juice." Mrs. Daniels leaned back and closed her eyes and sighed. "Do you know how to make coffee?"

"Yes. How do you like it?"

"Strong and with cream."

"What else would you like?"

"I would like a poached egg and a piece of lightly buttered toast." Mrs. Daniels opened her eyes. "Do you know how to do that?"

Christine nodded. "My dad likes poached eggs too."

Mrs. Daniels closed her eyes again. "Good."

Christine wandered through a spacious dining room with a long, dark table large enough to seat at least twelve. Along one wall of this room was a bank of French doors that looked out onto a perfectly landscaped backyard and what appeared to be an inground pool. Christine wondered if Mrs. Daniels actually used the pool, or was it just for looks? Then she went through a set of double swinging doors and found what she'd hoped for—a kitchen. And to Christine's surprise, it was a sunny-looking kitchen with walls the color of butter and light wood cabinets with glass doors. She ran her hand across the sleek granite countertops. A bit cool perhaps, but at least they were a pleasant color, a nice sandy tone that resembled the beach on a summer's day. She decided that so far this was her favorite room in the house.

She quickly located a juice glass, filled it, and took it to Mrs. Daniels. "Here," she said, worried that the old woman had fallen asleep. "You should probably drink this now. It's good for your blood sugar level."

Mrs. Daniels frowned. "What do you know about blood sugar levels?"

"My mother was a diabetic."

"Was? Oh yes, I do seem to remember that you mentioned she had passed on. When was that?"

38

"A few years ago." Christine looked away. This wasn't a subject she particularly cared to discuss with this woman.

"Yes, well, I'm sorry."

She nodded. "I'll get back to your breakfast now."

Christine was relieved to be back in the kitchen. Before long she had a poached egg, a slice of wheat toast, lightly buttered, and a hot cup of strong coffee, with cream. She placed these on a tray with silverware and a napkin, then took them to the living room.

"Did you want to eat in here?" she asked.

Mrs. Daniels shrugged. "I might as well. Although, normally, I frown upon such practices." She pointed to the glass-topped coffee table. "Put it there."

Christine returned to the kitchen to begin cleaning up. As she finished washing out the saucepan, she paused to look out the window over the sink and found herself staring at the large oak tree on the left side of the backyard. Something about its bare branches silhouetted against the pale gray sky held her attention in an almost haunting way. Then suddenly she realized that this house might have once been her biological mother's home. She wasn't sure how long Mrs. Daniels had lived here, but it seemed entirely possible that Lenore might have once stood right here at this very window, perhaps as a teen, and actually stared out at this very same tree.

She went back into the living room to see that Mrs. Daniels was finished. "More coffee?" she asked.

"Yes, please. And for future reference, you don't have to make it *that* strong."

"Sorry."

"Usually people make it too weak, so I always say strong. That was, however, too strong."

"Right." Christine picked up the tray and wondered if she would ever do anything to this woman's satisfaction.

"Everything else was all right."

"Thank you." Christine paused for a moment. "This is a lovely home, Mrs. Daniels. How long have you lived here?"

Mrs. Daniels frowned. "Oh, I'm not really sure. Let's see, James and I got married in 1980, and we moved in here shortly after that. You do the math."

Christine nodded and smiled. "A long time ago, anyway."

But as she walked back to the kitchen, it hit her full force that her mother had indeed lived here, walked upon these very floors, looked out of these actual windows. She wondered which room might have been Lenore's bedroom and if she might get to see it at some point. Also, she wondered about photos. So far she'd seen nothing. But why not? Oh, the questions that tumbled through her head as she refilled Mrs. Daniels's coffee cup. If only there was a way to get this cantankerous old woman to talk without revealing her true identity. Because, like it or not, the more Christine played this game and the deeper she got into it, the more she realized it would be difficult to step out of. Perhaps she would never be able to divulge the truth to her grandmother.

By noon Christine had done two loads of laundry and cleaned the downstairs bathrooms, Mrs. Daniels's bedroom, and the kitchen. She'd vacuumed and dusted the den and emptied all the trash receptacles. She continued to search for photos and clues while she worked, but so far she'd found nothing that seemed relevant to Lenore. Christine's chores were regularly interrupted by Mrs. Daniels, who was always asking for things like books, the newspaper, reading glasses, another cup of coffee, whatever seemed to strike her fancy at the moment. Plus, Christine was responsible for answering the phone and the door. And, for an older woman who lived alone, Mrs. Daniels seemed to have a lot of callers. Some of the phone calls were invitations to various luncheons and Christmas gatherings, all of which were declined, and the callers at the door were usually seeking donations or selling Christmas wreaths or delivering packages.

"This just came," Christine said as she handed Mrs. Daniels a box that was marked "Perishable."

"You can open any packages that come," Mrs. Daniels instructed. "Make sure you give me the card, then make a note of what's inside." She shook her head. "Christmas gifts can be such a bother."

Christine decided not to respond to that.

"Do you drive?" Mrs. Daniels asked suddenly.

"Drive?" Christine removed a fruit basket from the box. "A car, you mean?"

"Well, I wasn't referring to a golf cart."

Christine nodded. "Yes. My dad taught me to drive, but I don't have a car, if that's what you mean?"

"But you do have a driver's license?"

"Yes, of course."

"Good. I want you to take me somewhere."

"Do you want me to fix you some lunch first?"

"No, don't bother. We'll get something along the way."

Christine wondered what this woman was planning as she helped Mrs. Daniels get her coat and purse. But she knew better than to ask. Mrs. Daniels did not like to be questioned. Particularly by the hired help. Christine followed her out to the large three-car garage and helped her down the step, preparing herself to catch her if she started to fall.

"Wow," Christine said as she spotted the single car in the large garage. "You have a Jaguar."

Mrs. Daniels made a "humph" sound. "Not a very sensible choice either. I regret that I didn't keep the Mercedes instead. This car has been nothing but trouble."

"Trouble?" Christine ran her hand over its sleek silver surface.

"Mechanically speaking." Mrs. Daniels handed her the keys. "Of course, my mechanic loves me. Why, he even sends me a Christmas card each year. But then he could afford to send me fine jewelry for what he charges to fix this thing."

Christine opened the door for Mrs. Daniels and waited for the old woman to slowly arrange herself in the passenger seat before she closed the door. As Christine slid into the driver's seat, she noticed the faint smell of stale cigarette smoke. "Do you smoke?" she asked as she slid the key into the ignition. She instantly regretted her question and prepared herself to be chided again. To her surprise, Mrs. Daniels simply answered.

"Once in a while, but only when I'm feeling particularly stressed." She fumbled to fasten her seat belt. "But I've never smoked in the house. Can't abide the smell of smoke in a house, and it ruins the furniture and carpets.

Unfortunately, I used to smoke in the car. Quite a lot, as a matter of fact. I can't seem to get rid of the smell." She took a deep breath. "But I actually rather like it."

Christine thought that was a bit strange, but then a lot about this woman seemed strange. "Where are we going?"

"To the La-Z-Boy store. I want a comfortable chair."

Christine smiled to herself as she waited for the garage door to go up. It was interesting to imagine how a bulky recliner would fit into Mrs. Daniels's perfectly attired home with its fine Oriental carpets, valuable antiques, and original artwork. But it was plain to see this old woman was craving a little comfort in her old age. So despite what appeared to be Mrs. Daniels's style-dictated ways, Christine wondered if it might actually be possible to teach an old dog new tricks. And, if so, maybe the day would come when Christine could divulge her true identity.

5

"Where would you stop for a quick bite of lunch?" Mrs. Daniels asked as she peered out at the traffic zipping around town.

"Me?" Christine felt surprised. "Well, that would depend."

"On what?"

"A lot of things. Like whether I was alone or with a friend, or whether I was feeling flush or almost broke, or what I felt like eating. Remember, I'm a college student. I'm not above getting a buck burger when I'm starving and low on cash."

"What's a buck burger?"

"You know," Christine waited for the light to turn, "Whoppers for ninety-nine cents at Burger King. They're not bad, really."

"I thought you had worked for McDonald's. I'd think you'd be loyal to that establishment."

"Just because you work someplace doesn't mean you

like it." Christine hadn't meant it to sound like that. She glanced uneasily at Mrs. Daniels, worried that she'd make the connection, but it seemed to have floated right past her.

"Does this Burger King place have one of those windows where you can place an order without getting out?"

"Sure."

"Well, let's go there, then. I don't want to get out of the car." She slumped down into the seat.

"Are you all right?"

"Yes. I just don't want anyone I know to recognize me."

Christine laughed as she turned down the street toward Burger King. It took Mrs. Daniels a while to read the menu and decide on what she wanted, but finally they placed their order.

"That'll be seven forty-eight," said a grumpy voice through the intercom.

"Seven dollars and forty-eight cents?" Mrs. Daniels peered at Christine. "Can that possibly be right?"

"It sounds about right to me." Christine pulled the sleek car forward, careful to avoid the sign that seemed to stick right out into their lane. "Is it too much?"

Mrs. Daniels laughed. Only this time it didn't sound quite as cynical as it had yesterday. "Goodness, think of all the money I could've saved over the years if I'd eaten here. Of course, their food probably tastes like cardboard and glue."

To Christine's relief, Mrs. Daniels seemed to like her lunch. Although, when they were finished, she complained at the amount of cholesterol she'd just consumed.

45

"Oh, I suppose I shouldn't worry. I'm not long for this world anyway."

Christine glanced uneasily at the old woman. "Are you having health problems? Besides your ankle, I mean?"

She waved her hand. "Oh, nothing out of the ordinary. It's just that everything starts to go once you begin getting old. Don't know why people have to grow old, anyway. My two husbands certainly didn't bother with it."

At the La-Z-Boy store they were greeted with Christmas music, and a young blond woman dressed like an elf offered them store-bought cookies.

"Merry Christmas, it's our Holiday Blowout week," she told them in a chirpy voice. "Everything in the store is marked down, some up to 50 percent off, and ready to be delivered by Christmas."

"By Christmas?" Mrs. Daniels harped. "I need a chair and I need it now. Can't I have one delivered today?"

"Oh, I don't know," the woman said. "I—uh—"

"Hello, there," said a man in a khaki suit. "I'm Leon Myers. Now, what can I do for you today, ma'am?"

"I want a recliner chair," Mrs. Daniels said. "But I want it delivered before Christmas. I'd like it delivered today, if possible, or tomorrow at the latest."

He smiled. "No problem. If we have it in stock, we can deliver it by tomorrow."

"Fine, if that's the best you can do." She adjusted her crutches and moved forward. "Show me what you have."

"Looks like you've hurt your foot," the man said.

"Obviously," she snapped. "Why else would I want a recliner?"

He chuckled. "Oh, some people find our chairs to be

46

quite comfortable. Now, tell me, ma'am, will this chair be for you or for your husband?"

She rolled her eyes at Christine, as if to say, *This man is a complete idiot.* "It's for me. I need it to keep my foot elevated."

"Yes, yes, that's just what I thought." He paused by a pink velvet chair. "Now, how about this little number—"

"I can't stand pink," she snapped. "Show me something in an earth tone, please. And nothing too sleazy."

He chuckled again. "Oh, don't worry, ma'am. We have some real beauties." He led them over to a section of better-looking chairs, which also wore some more expensive price tags, Christine noticed.

However, Mrs. Daniels didn't seem to care. She pointed to a nice-looking tan chair by the wall. "I'll take that one," she said.

The salesman laughed. "Without even trying it out?"

"Why do I need to try it? Aren't they all the same?"

"No, no, they're all different. They're made to fit various body types and needs. I recommend you sit in it before you make up your mind."

"Fine." She hobbled around the maze of chairs until she reached the tan one. Then, holding her crutches out to the sides, she slowly leaned back and sat down with an "oomph." She reached for the small wooden handle on the side and after a bit of pulling finally managed to release the footrest. Then she put her head back and sighed. "This one suits me just fine. I'll take it."

The salesman grinned, and Christine suspected that, despite Mrs. Daniels's demanding ways, this had been one of his easiest transactions of the season. And Christine didn't disagree with the choice either. Of all the chairs, this one looked the least like a recliner. In fact, the sand-colored chenille fabric was rather soft and attractive. Christine wished she had enough money to get something like that for her father someday. She could imagine him putting his feet up after a long day. Maybe when he was finished with his missions work and she was done with school and had a real job, maybe then she could get him one.

Mrs. Daniels wrote out a check and inquired again as to the delivery.

"It's our busiest time of year," the woman behind the counter told her.

"I was promised that I would have it by tomorrow," she insisted.

The woman checked on the computer again. "We don't have anyone scheduled to deliver in your area until the end of the week."

"Well, if I can't have it by tomorrow, I simply won't purchase it today," Mrs. Daniels said firmly. "I'll just go to another store where—"

"Something wrong here?" Leon asked as he returned to the counter and looked at the woman who had written up the purchase.

"She wants it delivered by tomorrow," the woman said in a tired voice. "We don't have a truck going—"

"I told her it would be delivered tomorrow," Leon said, flashing a smile toward Mrs. Daniels. "And we expect it to be delivered tomorrow. Figure out a way to make it happen, Donna."

The woman scowled at him, then pushed some more

keys on her computer keyboard. "Fine. It'll be delivered by tomorrow. Do you plan to be home all day, ma'am?"

"I'm not exactly gadding about town with this bum foot," Mrs. Daniels said. "Of course I plan to be home. And if the chair's not delivered by tomorrow, I'll put a stop payment on my check."

"And a Merry Christmas to you too," the woman said as she wearily handed Mrs. Daniels the receipt.

Christine couldn't help but feel sorry for the woman as they headed for the exit.

"Happy Holidays!" the elf girl chirped.

"Yeah," Christine said as she opened the door for Mrs. Daniels. "To you too."

"Bah humbug," Mrs. Daniels said when they were out in the parking lot.

Christine glanced at the heavy clouds now filling the sky as she unlocked the car. "Do you think it's going to snow this year?" she asked once they were inside. "I'd love to see a white Christmas."

"Good grief! I certainly hope not. I already ruined my ankle from slipping on my wet patio. Now all I need is snow on the ground with these crutches and I could probably end up in a body cast for the entire holidays."

Christine noticed a Christmas tree lot as she pulled into traffic. "Do you plan to get a Christmas tree?"

"Of course not. What on earth would I do with a Christmas tree? Do you expect me to hobble around and decorate it?"

"I could decorate it."

"I don't put up a tree anymore. I haven't since the kids left. That's when my husband and I began going down to

Palm Springs for the holidays. This will be the first year I've been forced to stay at home."

"So why don't you have your stepson or grandchildren over for Christmas?"

She harrumphed. "Not if I can help it."

"What do you do, then?"

Christine could feel Mrs. Daniels glaring at her, and she suspected she'd pushed her too far by asking way too many questions. The old woman cleared her throat, then spoke in a sharp voice. "I plan to do as little as possible for the holidays. I suppose someone like you would think I was a real Ebenezer Scrooge. And maybe I am. But then that's my business."

Christine nodded and continued driving in silence until they reached Mrs. Daniels's home.

"Furthermore," Mrs. Daniels remained in the car as she continued speaking, as if they'd still been in the midst of a conversation. "I have hired you to be my housekeeper and errand girl. I do not expect you to be my companion."

Christine felt tears burning in her eyes, but she was determined not to show this thoughtless woman how her words were able to cut. She opened the passenger door and helped her get out of the low car and then into the house.

After getting Mrs. Daniels settled comfortably on the couch for an afternoon nap, Christine busied herself by washing the windows in the kitchen. It looked as if they hadn't been washed in ages. And as she washed them she wondered about her birth mother. Had Lenore ever washed these windows? Or had they always been the kind of family to hire out their household chores? Christine couldn't imagine having enough money to pay other people to do things like this. And even if she did, she couldn't imagine wanting to. Something about manual labor and taking something that was once dirty and making it clean appealed to her. She always felt better when it was done. She realized that this work ethic probably wasn't genetic, but rather a trait she'd been taught by her hardworking parents. More than ever she felt thankful for them now. And more than ever she missed her father's warmth and kind, loving support.

6

By the second day "on the job," Christine felt she was falling into something of a rhythm. At least it seemed so to her. Mrs. Daniels, on the other hand, seemed to enjoy stirring things up a bit by changing her mind about things like how she liked her coffee or the best way to dust the antique furniture. Still, Christine was trying to be patient. But by four o'clock, two things happened that just about undid her. First the deliveryman arrived with the recliner. And that was not so bad, but just as he was setting the rather bulky chair in the center of the living room, Mrs. Daniels's daughter-in-law, Felicity, showed up quite unexpectedly.

"Why is there a La-Z-Boy truck in your driveway?" she demanded as soon as she was in the door.

Mrs. Daniels turned and stared at her. "Well, hello to you too, Felicity."

"What's going on?" Felicity asked when she saw the

deliveryman removing the plastic wrappings from the chair.

"What does it look like?" Mrs. Daniels asked in an exasperated voice. "I've purchased a recliner."

"A recliner?"

"That's what they call them." Mrs. Daniels glanced over to where Christine was looking on without speaking. "And I'd like you to meet my new housekeeper, Christine Bradley. Christine, this is my stepson's wife, Felicity Daniels."

Felicity moved her attention from the recliner to Christine. "Aren't you a little young to be a housekeeper?"

"I'm nearly twenty."

"Oh. Well, do you have much experience doing—"

"Felicity," Mrs. Daniels interrupted. "I am the one who hired Christine, and she works for me. I am perfectly capable of ascertaining her qualifications, thank you very much."

"Well, I—"

"And what brings you here this time of day, anyway? Shouldn't you be picking up the children or something?"

"They're at my mother's."

Mrs. Daniels seemed to stiffen a bit. "Of course."

"Well, that's it," the deliveryman said as he gathered up a bundle of plastic. "You wanna try her out before I leave?"

Mrs. Daniels frowned at him, then seemed to think better of his suggestion. "Yes, as a matter of fact, I will." She hobbled over and eased herself down, tested the leg rest, then leaned back and nodded. "It's just fine. Thank you."

"Merry Christmas, ma'am," the man said. He hesitated

for a moment, and Christine wondered if he expected a tip or something. But finally he just backed out and left.

"Is that where you're going to leave it?" Felicity asked. "Right in the middle of the room like that?"

"Maybe." Mrs. Daniels smiled smugly. It was plain that she enjoyed irritating her daughter-in-law. Then she turned to Christine. "I'd like a cup of tea, please. The same kind you made for me yesterday will be fine."

Christine glanced at Felicity. "Would you like a cup too?"

Felicity flopped down on the couch across from her mother-in-law. "Sure, why not."

Mrs. Daniels didn't look pleased. "So what brings you by today, Felicity?"

Christine couldn't hear the rest of their conversation from the kitchen, but she hurried to make the tea and returned quickly with a tray, complete with a small dish of some chocolate mint cookies she'd spied in the pantry. She set it down on the glass coffee table between them. Then she took her time handing Mrs. Daniels her tea and offering her the cookies.

"I already told you that I have no plans for the holidays," Mrs. Daniels said. "What's so unusual about that?"

"I just don't understand it," Felicity said. "You have this big, beautiful home. And it would be so lovely to decorate it for Christmas." She pointed toward the staircase. "I can just imagine that banister strewn with evergreen garlands—"

"I do not want my banister strewn with evergreen garlands, thank you very much."

"What about a tree over by the fireplace. Your ceilings are so tall that you could have a ten-foot—"

"I do not want a ten-foot tree, Felicity, any more than I want a ten-inch tree. What is it about no that you don't understand?"

Felicity frowned and set her cup down with a clink. "I would think you'd do it, at least for your grandchildren. Give them some memories—"

"Felicity," Mrs. Daniels began in a very stern voice. "I know you well enough to know that it's not for the children. If I opened my home to a Christmas party, as you call it, it would only be to impress your family and friends. If you want to have a Christmas party, have it at your own house."

"But I would do all the work—"

"And I would foot the bill."

Felicity's face puckered up now. Whether she was going to cry or explode was anyone's guess, but Christine suspected by the way she was glaring at her that she'd already overstayed her welcome.

"Can I get you anything else?" she asked as she prepared to make a hasty exit.

"No, thank you, Christine, this is fine," Mrs. Daniels said in a surprisingly polite voice.

Christine returned to the kitchen but lingered by the door, hoping to hear a few more snippets of conversation. And to her pleased surprise, the long dining room worked almost like an echo chamber. Sure, she felt a bit guilty for eavesdropping, but then, whether they knew it or not, she was actually part of this family. Didn't she have some right to know about the goings-on here?

"Well, fine," Felicity said in a sharp voice. "If that's the way you're going to be about it."

"That's right."

"Well, I suppose you won't want to trouble yourself to come over for Jamie's birthday either? Poor kid, it's bad enough having a birthday in December, but I suppose you're going to let your injury keep you from—"

"I still plan to come over for Jamie's birthday. Isn't the party on Friday?"

A few more words were said, and then it sounded like Felicity was leaving. After a bit Christine returned to the living room to pick up the tray of tea things.

"Looks like we'll need to do a little shopping tomorrow," Mrs. Daniels said as Christine loaded up the tray.

"Shopping?"

"Yes. My grandson is having his seventh birthday on Friday. Do you have any idea what a seven-year-old might like?"

"I used to baby-sit for a couple of little boys who just loved Legos. And they collected all these amazing sets, like clipper ships and space shuttles. They'd play with them for hours."

"Legos?" She nodded. "Might be just the trick."

So, on the following morning, after the basic routine was completed, Christine drove Mrs. Daniels to the toy store at the mall. Of course, the parking lot was packed, and after driving around several times, Christine finally decided to drop Mrs. Daniels at the door.

"I don't see why you don't just park in the handicapped space," Mrs. Daniels complained as Christine helped her out of the car.

"You don't have a permit," Christine said for the third time.

"Permit shermit."

"I'll be back in a few minutes."

Christine found Mrs. Daniels waiting at the door, clearly aggravated by the potbellied man clanging a bell as he solicited donations.

"Do they think they'll make money by irritating the shoppers?" she asked as Christine held the door open for her.

They circumvented the crowded "Take Your Photo with Santa" display, complete with stuffed reindeer, elves, and fake snow, as they made their way toward the nearby toy store. The sounds of children laughing and shouting, and some even crying, mixed with the tinny sound of Christmas music being played over the PA system. After working their way through the holiday shoppers crowding the toy store, which was naturally having a big holiday sale, they finally located the right section. And after examining the various sets of Legos, Mrs. Daniels decided on the Extreme Tower building set. It had been Christine's recommendation, although she hadn't realized it was so expensive, but Mrs. Daniels seemed happy to think it was her own idea. And Christine didn't mind. She was just thankful to get out of there before Mrs. Daniels's mood or energy level deteriorated.

"Do you mind waiting while I bring the car around?" Christine asked.

"I suppose I could sit on this bench in here," she grumbled. "That way I can avoid the neurotic bell ringer outside."

Christine smiled. "That's a good idea." Then, carrying the bulky package, she jogged across the parking lot to the car.

"I don't know what I'll do about Christmas shopping this year," Mrs. Daniels said after she was seated comfortably back in the car.

"You buy Christmas presents?" Christine felt mildly surprised.

Mrs. Daniels cackled. "Well, I may be a Scrooge about all the trappings and trimmings, but I'm not cheap when it comes to gifts. I certainly don't want my grandchildren growing up thinking I was stingy."

"You could shop online," Christine suggested.

"You mean on a computer?"

"Yeah. It's really pretty convenient. You can find anything."

"Anything?"

"Pretty much." Christine waited in a long line of traffic trying to get out of the parking lot.

"Even people?"

"Huh?" Christine glanced over at Mrs. Daniels, who seemed to be deep in thought. "You want to buy your grandkids some people?"

"No, of course not. But I've heard you can use the Internet to locate people. Is that correct?"

"Sure. There are all kinds of ways to search."

"And you know how to use a computer?"

"Yeah. I've been using one for years."

"But I don't have a computer."

"You could get one," Christine suggested as she finally made her way onto the street.

"I suppose I could. Of course, I wouldn't have any idea of what to look for or where to go. Would you?"

Christine pointed across the street to Computer World.

"That's a pretty good place right there. My roommate just got a great deal on a laptop."

"What's that?"

Before Christine could even finish her explanation, Mrs. Daniels interrupted. "That's what I want too, Christine. Stop in there and let's get one."

Christine grinned as she put on her turn signal. This woman might be a little grumpy, but she was certainly entertaining. Fortunately, Computer World was not as busy as the mall, and Christine found a space right in front.

Mrs. Daniels leaned back her head and sighed. "The problem is that I'm exhausted from our toy shopping."

"Do you want to go home?"

"Not without a computer." Mrs. Daniels opened her purse and removed her Visa card. "Here, you go pick out the one you think will best suit me."

"Are you sure?"

"Of course," she snapped. "Just hurry."

Feeling a bit strange, Christine went in and purchased the same computer that Brianna had bragged about just a month ago. She was all ready for the high-school-age salesclerk to question her signature on Mrs. Daniels's credit card, but he didn't seem to notice or care. He was probably just happy to make such an easy sale. The store didn't appear overly busy, and she suspected the salesclerks worked on commission.

"Merry Christmas!" he yelled as she carried the box out the door.

"Merry Christmas," she called back.

Mrs. Daniels was fast asleep and snoring quietly when Christine opened the car door to let herself in. Saying nothing, Christine started the engine and headed for home. She glanced over at her silent passenger while waiting at a stoplight and noticed how much softer the old woman's face looked when she was sleeping. She almost did look like someone's grandmother. A wave of longing swept over Christine. Suddenly she wished she could tell this woman who she was and why she was here. But then she remembered the old woman's warning about no shenanigans. How would Mrs. Daniels react to the news that she'd been tricked like this, deceived by her own granddaughter?

7

"Do you recall that I said you'll be required to work some evenings?" Mrs. Daniels asked on Friday morning.

"Yes," Christine said as she helped Mrs. Daniels from the shower.

"Well, I need you to drive me over to my stepson's house. It's my grandson Jamie's birthday party this evening, and I promised to come. And, if you don't mind, you could just stick around and then take me home afterward. I know it's an inconvenience for you, but I don't plan to stay late. Naturally, I will pay you extra. I don't expect you to work for nothing."

"It's okay," Christine said as she carefully rebandaged the injured foot. "And you don't need to pay me extra. I'm glad to do it as a favor."

"Nonsense." Mrs. Daniels firmly shook her head. "How do you ever expect to get ahead in this world if you talk like that?"

"Money isn't everything," Christine said as she finished

the last wrap and pinned it securely. She stood up and smiled. "But I'm sure you know that."

She frowned. "Goodness, I hope you're not going to preach a sermon at me now."

Christine shrugged as she gathered the wet towels. "Sorry, I'm not much of a preacher."

Due to the festivities planned for the evening, Mrs. Daniels decided they would have a quiet day at home. They'd gone grocery shopping yesterday, and Mrs. Daniels was still learning how to use her new computer. Christine had started her out by teaching her how to play some of the card games so she could get comfortable with the keyboard and mouse, and later on today she'd show her how to cruise the Internet.

"Would you wrap Jamie's gift for me?" Mrs. Daniels said that afternoon. "There are wrapping things in that high cupboard in the laundry room."

"I'd be happy to," Christine said as she picked up the empty teacup from the side table she'd moved next to the new recliner. "I love wrapping gifts."

Mrs. Daniels seemed to consider this as she picked up her book. "I used to enjoy wrapping gifts too. Then my daughter took over for me, and, well, I guess I never really did it much after that."

Christine felt an unexpected tightness across her chest, almost as if someone had wrapped a wide leather belt there and then suddenly cinched it. It was the first time Mrs. Daniels had made any mention of a daughter.

"You have a daughter?" Christine said, hoping to sound only mildly interested.

Mrs. Daniels sighed. "I used to."

"Oh."

Mrs. Daniels pulled out the footrest and leaned back. "I think I'll rest now. You'd better take care of that gift. And see if you can find a birthday card. I keep a box in the second drawer down on my desk."

It was obvious that Christine wasn't going to extract any other information about Lenore just now. So she went on her way and discovered a very nice selection of gift wrap and bows in the cupboard above the dryer. She suspected these items had been there for a long time. Maybe even back when Lenore lived here. Christine selected a blue and white paper with sailboats. It seemed boyish, even if it was a bit old-fashioned. Then she carefully wrapped the box, taking time to neatly fold under the seams and create a large red and white bow to go on top. *Not bad*, she thought as she carried it into the kitchen.

Next she went to the desk where she usually sorted and set the daily mail. She'd never opened a drawer before. To her, a desk seemed a private place, and something a person should never go snooping in. As instructed, she pulled open the second drawer down and saw embossed stationery and envelopes and stamps and even some postcards and pretty note cards. But no box of greeting cards. She decided to try the next drawer down. Surely, this couldn't be considered snooping. But that drawer revealed only some old, yellowed typing paper and notepads with the university logo on them. Maybe the box was in the bottom drawer. She felt slightly guilty as she tried the drawer. She knew she was looking for more than birthday cards now, but she couldn't stop herself. The drawer stuck at first, but with a harder pull it came open.

There, lying face down in the mostly empty drawer, was what appeared to be a framed photo. She knew she should close the drawer immediately, that she had definitely crossed over the line and this would be considered snooping, but it was too late. Glancing over her shoulder once, she picked up the frame, then turned it over and stared in astonishment.

The pretty brunette girl in the picture had to be Lenore. Christine had never seen a picture of her birth mother before (her father had explained that Lenore had claimed to be camera shy and never allowed them to take even one photo). Just the same, Christine instinctively knew this young woman had to be her birth mother. It was probably a high school graduation picture. And it wasn't so much that the woman in the photo looked like Christine, although she sensed a familiarity in the eyes. They were brown and big and had another quality she couldn't even be certain of. But everything else about the two young women seemed to be different. Where Lenore's hair was dark and straight, Christine's was auburn and much too wavy. Their faces were entirely different too. Lenore had a sweetly rounded face with a cute little nose, where Christine's face was more angular and her nose straight and narrow and, in her opinion, slightly too long. Not so unlike Mrs. Daniels's. Christine heard a sound and quickly replaced the photo, closed the stubborn drawer, then stood up with heart pounding fast.

She waited a full minute before she moved. Then, walking casually toward the living room, she prepared herself for Mrs. Daniels's accusations and questions. But the old woman was still asleep in her recliner, snoring peacefully.

Probably as an act of penance, Christine got out the mop and bucket and gave the kitchen floor a good cleaning. She felt guilty and nervous about her snooping, but at the same time she didn't completely regret it. Even though it was unsettling to look into the eyes of the woman who had birthed her, it seemed right too. After all, Lenore was her mother. Didn't she have every right to know what the young woman had looked like? She knew so little about her short and tragic life. Suddenly Christine felt hungry to know more. But how could she find anything out when her grandmother was so reluctant to talk? And how could she go around snooping and still live with herself?

Christine scrubbed hard as she considered ways to find things out and how she might get her grandmother to open up and talk about her daughter. She paused as she rinsed out the mop. When had she quit thinking of that old woman in there as "Mrs. Daniels" and begun considering her a grandmother? Perhaps it had to do with seeing the photo of Lenore. Or maybe Christine was actually becoming fond of the cranky old woman. Whatever it was, she decided not to think about it too much. She poured out the dirty mop water and turned to see the tile floor gleaming as a result of her energetic scrub down. Perhaps this would help cleanse her conscience a bit too.

It was almost five now and the time when she usually set out her grandmother's dinner and then said good-night and headed back to her dorm. But since she was taking Mrs. Daniels to the birthday party, she was unsure as to what she should do. After her mopping spree, she suddenly felt as if she really should run back to her dorm and change before the party, but then she wasn't sure what

65

time they needed to leave, or even how far away the house was. Why hadn't she thought of this sooner?

"What are you doing in there?" Mrs. Daniels called from the dining room.

Christine poked her head out of the swinging doors. "I just finished some mopping. Don't come in here though, the floor's still damp, you might slip." She put the mop and bucket back in the laundry room closet and went back to check on her grandmother.

"Mopping?" the old woman said as she sat up straight in her chair.

"It looked like it needed it."

"I suppose it did."

"Do you want me to fix you a bite to eat before I leave?"

"Leave?" she looked alarmed. "Where are you going?"

"I thought maybe I could run back to my dorm and change before it's time to go."

"But we should be leaving for the party in about twenty minutes, and I need you to help me change."

"Well, do you want me to fix you something to eat, then?"

"Didn't I tell you it's a dinner party?"

"A dinner party for a seven-year-old?"

"Well, they had the kiddy party this afternoon," she explained. "They always invite their grown-up friends and relatives over in the evening for another party." She laughed in that cynical way. "Ensures the kids get more gifts that way."

"Oh."

So Christine stayed and helped Mrs. Daniels get dressed

in a pair of black knit pants and a burgundy velvet jacket. "You look really nice," she told her when they were finally done.

Mrs. Daniels patted her hair. "Best I can do under the circumstances." She frowned at Christine. "Is that what you're wearing?"

Christine looked down at her gray sweatshirt and jeans. "Well, I thought maybe I'd have time to go home and change, but then the party was earlier than I thought . . ."

"Well, it just won't do. Felicity is, shall we say, a bit of a snob." She rolled her eyes. "She likes for people to dress and act right. Especially at her little parties. Now go in there and look in my closet. I'm sure my trousers would be too big for you, but see if you can find a different shirt to wear. Something that looks respectable. Choose whatever you like, I don't care."

Christine tried not to show her displeasure at this task. The last thing she wanted to do right now was to don some fuddy-duddy old lady shirt. But she felt bad that she hadn't planned ahead better and decided that she should at least be cooperative. She hunted for a bit until she found a rust-colored turtleneck sweater that wasn't too bad. She held it out to show Mrs. Daniels, who was waiting comfortably in the easy chair by the window.

"How about this?"

"That should look good on you. Will go nicely with your hair."

Christine went back into the closet and slipped it on to discover it was quite soft and cozy. She emerged with a self-conscious smile. "It fits okay."

"Better than it fits me, I suspect." Mrs. Daniels pushed

herself up from the chair and fumbled for her crutches. "In fact, you should just keep it. That color makes me look too sallow anyway. Something I don't need at this stage of life." She chuckled. "I will say this for you though. For a girl without money, you certainly have good taste."

"Huh?" Christine was walking behind her down the hallway.

"Cashmere," Mrs. Daniels said. "Imported from France."

Suddenly Christine felt terrible. "Oh, I'm sorry. You should've told me. I can't keep this, I'll go—"

"No. Like I said, the color does nothing for me. My late husband got that for me for Christmas one year when rust was all the rage."

"Are you sure?"

"Positive."

Mrs. Daniels stopped by the large coat closet by the door. "And while we're at it, there's a coat in there that you might like to have too. As I recall it went nicely with the sweater. Go ahead and open it. It's a suede jacket in a brownish gold tone that looks awful on me."

Christine looked in the mostly empty coat closet, then spied a caramel-colored suede jacket behind a hooded rain parka. She pulled it out. "Is this it?"

"Yes. I've been meaning to give it away. Can't stand how it makes me look. Go ahead, try it on."

Christine slipped on the jacket. The suede was so smooth that it felt like butter. And she suspected by the luxurious satin lining and fancy label that it must've been very expensive. "It's beautiful."

"It's yours." She looked at her watch. "We better go. Doesn't do to keep Felicity waiting."

Christine almost felt like a princess as she drove Mrs. Daniels's Jaguar, dressed in the cashmere sweater and suede jacket. She wondered what Brianna, or even her dad, would think of her right now.

"That's the housing development," Mrs. Daniels said. "Aspen Grove."

Christine didn't say anything, but she was surprised. This didn't seem like a very impressive neighborhood for the way her grandmother had described Felicity. It was nice, of course, and probably much more expensive than the neighborhood Christine had grown up in. But even in the night, with only the streetlights to illuminate, all the houses appeared to look alike, and they were so close together it seemed like neighbors could reach out their windows and hold hands. Of course, she didn't mention this.

"You're here," said a tall man as he opened the door wider. "Come on in, Mom. Is that your caregiver with you?"

"Housekeeper," Mrs. Daniels corrected him in a stern voice.

"Let me help you," he said as he tried to usher her inside.

"No, you just stay back, Jimmy. I can do this better on my own."

"Getting pretty feisty with those crutches, aren't you?" He turned and winked at Christine. "She's a handful, isn't she?"

Christine wasn't quite sure how to respond. So she stuck out her hand and said, "Hi, I'm Christine Bradley." She stopped herself from saying, *Lenore's long lost daughter.*

"Well, welcome to our humble abode, Christine. I'm Jimmy. I hear that you've already met my wife, Felicity, and—"

"Who's that?" asked a little boy peering out from behind his dad. He had curly red hair and was eyeing the large gift in Christine's hands.

"This is Christine," Jimmy said. "And this is the birthday boy, Jamie."

She smiled. "Hello, Jamie. Happy birthday. Kind of a bummer having a birthday so close to Christmas, isn't it?"

He grinned to reveal a missing tooth. "Yeah. Some people give you only one present and say that it's for both."

"Well, this is for you from your grandma," Christine said as she handed him the large box.

His eyes grew wide. "Cool."

Soon she met the other child, a little girl named Casey. And despite their grandmother's less than favorable description, Christine thought they were sweet kids, even if they were fairly rambunctious. Casey had blond hair and blue eyes like her mother, while Jamie resembled his dad. And both children insisted on showing Christine their rooms. Maybe it was because she was the closest to their age group, or maybe they just assumed she was the babysitter. As it turned out, she spent more time with the kids than the adults, which was perfectly fine with her.

She sat next to Casey at dinner. The other guests consisted of Felicity's parents, Janet and George, and her newly married sister, Amber, and Amber's husband, Rick.

"Do you go to college here?" Amber asked.

"Yes. I'm a junior," Christine said.

"I graduated from here," Amber said. Then, more proudly, "But Rick went to Stanford."

"I went to school here too," Jimmy said. "It's a great place to go."

"What was your major?" Christine asked, only because it seemed the conversation had come to a lull.

"Secondary education," he said. "I'm a P.E. teacher at Edison High."

"And a coach," Felicity added.

"I'm majoring in education too," Christine said. "Elementary ed."

"Good grief," Mrs. Daniels said with a frown. "You seemed like you were smarter than that to me. What's wrong with these young people wanting to waste their lives being teachers?" She seemed to direct this comment to Felicity's parents. "Don't young people care about making a good living anymore?"

"Thanks a lot, Mom," Jimmy said. "But don't forget that my dad was in education and so were you."

"*Upper* education," Mrs. Daniels corrected him. "I was an English professor, and the head of my department before I retired. And don't forget that your father had his doctorate. As did my first husband."

"And I'm sure they're terribly thankful about that now," Jimmy teased.

Christine thought she saw her grandmother wince slightly at that.

"Sorry, Mom," Jimmy said quickly. "I guess I'm just saying that everyone's got to do what makes them happy. Life isn't just about making money, you know."

"My father's a teacher too," Christine said quickly, hoping to smooth over whatever had just transpired. "Actually, he retired from public school last spring. But he's volunteer teaching down in Brazil right now."

Fortunately, that took the conversation into a whole new realm as Felicity's parents enthusiastically shared their latest trip to Mexico.

Soon dinner was over and it was time for the gifts to be opened. Naturally, all this attention for her older brother was upsetting to Casey, and before long she was in tears.

"It's been a long day," Felicity explained, "and she never got her nap."

"Would you like me to help her get ready for bed?" Christine offered.

Felicity looked surprised then relieved. "Would you?"

"Sure, if she doesn't mind." She turned to look at the little girl's tear-streaked face. "Would you like to show me your room again, Casey? And where you keep your jammies?"

Casey nodded, and Christine took her hand and walked her up the stairs to her bedroom. It didn't take long before she was ready for bed, and although she looked pretty tired, Christine asked her if she'd like to hear a story.

"A book?" Casey's eyes grew wide as if this were a special treat.

"Yeah. Want me to read to you?"

She nodded and leaned back into her pillow, tugging a stuffed bunny closer to her. Christine took the bunny as a cue and picked out a rabbit story. Casey listened happily but was fast asleep before the story was half finished. Christine set the book down and pushed a stray blond curl off the little girl's forehead. She knew this child was no relation to her, but she felt an inexplicable sense of kinship just now. Maybe it had to do with Christmastime or missing her father. Or maybe she was just longing for a family of her own, people who loved her and really belonged to her.

"How'd it go?" a male voice whispered from the hallway.

She looked up to see Jimmy with his son in his arms. "Good," she told him. "Poor thing, she really was tired."

"So's the birthday boy."

Christine smiled. "Do you want me to put him to bed too?"

Jimmy shook his head. "I got it covered. Thanks though."

So Christine went back downstairs to where the adults had gathered in the small living room.

"We're getting our Christmas tree tomorrow," Felicity announced. "Jimmy doesn't like getting it before Jamie's birthday. But it always feels late with only a week left until Christmas. Most people have had their trees up for ages by now."

"And you're still planning on having everyone over for Christmas Eve?" Janet asked. "It'll be quite a full house for you."

Felicity sighed. "Well, you guys don't have much space since you scaled down to the condo and motor home. And Amber and Rick's apartment is pretty tiny. So I guess it's up to me."

"Is Jimmy's aunt still planning to come?" Janet asked.

"What?" Mrs. Daniels looked somewhat shocked.

Christine studied her grandmother, curious as to why she would be upset by this news.

"Aunt Hattie," Jimmy explained. "She wants to come visit during the holidays. She hasn't seen the kids in a couple of years."

Mrs. Daniels groaned. "My, how time flies."

Christine noticed Felicity nudging Jimmy with her elbow. It was a small gesture and probably not noticed by anyone else. But the expression on Felicity's face looked urgent.

Jimmy cleared his throat. "In fact . . . ," he said, "we were wondering if you might be able to put the old girl up for a couple of days—"

"What?" Mrs. Daniels demanded.

Jimmy smiled hopefully. "Otherwise she'll have to sleep on the couch, and that's not very comfortable. You have so much room, Mom. Surely you could let bygones be bygones this one time. You know, you ladies aren't getting any younger. Besides that, it's Christmas."

"You honestly think Hattie would be willing to stay at *my* house?" Mrs. Daniels narrowed her eyes. "You know that the last time we spoke was at your father's funeral."

"People often say things they don't mean during times of grief," Janet offered, obviously trying to smooth things over.

"I suppose Jimmy has told you the Aunt Hattie story," Mrs. Daniels said in a droll tone. "I suppose the whole town knows the Aunt Hattie story."

Christine wanted to raise her hand and say, *I don't.* But she wisely kept her peace, knowing it would look suspicious for Mrs. Daniels's housekeeper to be curious about

74

some estranged aunt. Just the same, she did wonder if this woman might be related to her.

"I told Felicity's family only so they could be prepared for any fireworks between you two." Jimmy smiled at Christine now. "You probably wonder what on earth we're talking about, don't you?"

She shrugged. "Oh, that's all right."

"Aunt Hattie is my dad's sister. And she said some things to my stepmom at his funeral that Mom's never forgiven her for."

"That's enough," Mrs. Daniels snapped.

"Please, Mom," Jimmy pleaded. "Couldn't you consider having Aunt Hattie for a few days? I mean, she is Dad's sister. Doesn't she deserve a little respect for that?"

Mrs. Daniels rolled her eyes. "Fine. She can stay at my house. But she better not expect me to cater to her. I'm not exactly in tip-top form, you know."

"But you have Christine," Felicity said hopefully. "I'm sure she can do whatever it takes to help make Aunt Hattie feel welcome."

"Of course," Christine said. "That's no problem at all."

"Any other surprise visitors you'd like to spring on me?" Mrs. Daniels glared at Jimmy.

He laughed. "No, Mom, that's it."

"Now if I can just figure where we'll put everyone for the Christmas party," Felicity said. It seemed an obvious hint.

Janet frowned. "That's too bad about your foot, Esther. Otherwise, you might want to have been able to host the gathering at your house."

Christine glanced at Mrs. Daniels in time to see her bristle.

"Yes, it's a shame. But as you can see, I have difficulty doing much of anything these days. A Christmas get-together would be completely out of the question."

"That is, unless you wanted to put me to work," Christine offered. She instantly wondered what on earth had prompted her to make such a bold offer. She saw her grandmother's eyebrows lifting and knew she'd stepped way over the line this time. But after seeing how small Felicity and Jimmy's house was, she could almost understand their dilemma. "It was just an idea," she said quietly.

"It's a great idea," Felicity said with a bright smile. "And I would help with everything too."

"Well, there you go," Janet said with a twinkle in her eye. "Looks like you're fresh out of excuses, Esther."

Mrs. Daniels scowled at Christine, but then to everyone's surprise she said, "Oh, I suppose I might as well give in. You're all ganging up against me anyway. But don't expect me to lift a finger."

"Oh, you won't have to, Mom," Felicity gushed. "Christine and I will handle everything. Won't we, Christine?"

Christine nodded, wondering what she'd gotten herself into. She hadn't really intended to coerce the old woman into opening up her home for the holidays. She knew it could totally backfire on her. But perhaps it had simply been her subconscious mind at work, making sure that she was included in this odd family during the holidays. Of course, she had no idea if they would even want her around. It seemed more than likely that they would simply expect her to play the role of housekeeper and then make herself scarce. Well, whatever, she'd already stuck her foot in her mouth.

"I hope you know what you've gotten yourself into," her grandmother said as they drove home.

"I'm so sorry, Mrs. Daniels," she began. "It just slipped out. And if it makes you feel any better, I don't want you to pay me for anything I do to get ready for Felicity's party. I want it to be my gift."

"First of all, I don't want you to keep calling me *Mrs. Daniels*. My students always called me *Professor* Daniels, and my friends just call me Esther. I've never been too fond of *Mrs. Daniels*, it sounds so matronly. Please, just call me Esther."

"Well, okay."

"And the second thing. I don't like hearing all this talk about not being paid. I am not a charity case, Christine. And I've never cheated anyone out of what is their just due. If you do a job well, you should be paid well."

"What if I mess it up?"

Esther laughed, but it was her cynical laugh. "Then I suppose you'll get what you deserve."

"That's what I'm afraid of," Christine said in a quiet voice. So quiet that she suspected her grandmother hadn't even heard.

8

To her own surprise, Esther wished Christine was around to help her prepare for bed. Not that she'd had too much trouble with that lately. It had helped a great deal when Christine had started laying out her bed things, everything right where she could reach it after she sat down. Why, the girl even went to the effort of placing a glass of ice water on her bedside table, along with a pain pill on a little china saucer, just in case she needed it. Which she usually did not. Not only that, but the girl had even begun turning down her bed for her lately. Just like in a nice hotel. Next thing, she'd probably be putting a chocolate on her pillow. Esther chuckled to herself as she pulled on her pajama top.

And yet, despite all this good service, there was something about the girl that disturbed Esther. She couldn't quite put her finger on it. But something just didn't feel right. It was like the old adage "If it sounds too good to be true . . ." Somehow Esther suspected this might be the case with this Christine Bradley. If that was her real name. One couldn't be too careful these days. She had just read about an elderly woman getting swindled in a bank deal. The old lady had been befriended by a young handyman who had worked for her a few days. After gaining her trust, he'd told her that his father was trying to transfer some money to him so he could rent an apartment, but the bank wouldn't accept the transfer unless he opened an account and deposited enough money to cover the transfer. Naturally, "enough money" had amounted to several thousand dollars. Several thousand dollars the poor old woman would never see again. People prey on the elderly, Esther reminded herself as she eased into bed.

Still, Christine didn't exactly seem like a scam artist to her. Although you can never be too sure, she told herself. Kids were sharp these days, and everyone has an angle. She just wished she could figure out what Christine's was. She seemed too smart of a girl to be stuck living in a college dorm during the holidays, then working as a housekeeper, of all things. Why, other kids her age were probably off doing exciting things like skiing in the mountains or sunning down in Florida or whatever it was that college kids did these days. More and more it seemed that young people had become a bit of a foreign commodity to her. The last young person to live in her home had been Lenore. And even she'd been something of a mystery. Then, to make matters worse, just consider what her own daughter had done to her. Well, maybe she'd better watch out for herself with Christine. Maybe she just shouldn't trust young people at all.

She laid her head back on the pillow and sighed. Still,

she had to admit she liked the girl. And despite her misgivings and suspicions, this particular girl had a way of growing on a person. But perhaps that was simply the result of Esther's temporary handicap. She'd read accounts of victims, people who had been kidnapped by hoodlums, but after a while they learned to love and actually trust their ruthless captors. She thought it was called Stockholm syndrome, but she wasn't positive. Perhaps that was happening to her with this caregiver or housekeeper or whatever it was she'd been trying to classify Christine as.

It was hard being needy like this. But, in reality, it wasn't going to get any better in the coming years. Good grief, she'd be eighty soon. She'd never intended to live this long, to outlive two husbands and wind up all alone like this. She didn't like feeling so vulnerable and defenseless. And to be so dependent, and to have to rely on a perfect stranger like this. Well, it was downright discomfiting, and she'd be highly relieved when this nonsense was all over and done and she could be back on her own two feet again. Although her doctor had said that wouldn't be until after New Year's.

Despite her worries, Esther smiled to herself in the darkness. She'd been surprised at how easily Christine had interacted with Jimmy's kids. It was rather sweet, really, and perhaps a sign that the girl wasn't of a criminal character after all. Didn't they say that children and animals had good instincts about people? Of course, Esther had never had a knack for children herself and it didn't mean that she was a bad person. Surely, it was simply the result of growing up as an only child. But then if she remembered correctly, it seemed that Christine had been an only child too. But then Christine was majoring in elementary education, so of course she'd be comfortable around children. She obviously just had a natural affinity for them. Well, some people were like that. Some were not. She definitely was not.

Christine, Christine, Christine. She should have something better to think about than that silly girl. It was as if she was becoming obsessed with this young woman. And what was the sense in that? This was a temporary arrangement at best. Good grief, for all she knew the girl might not even show up tomorrow. And even so, Christine would return to her classes after the New Year, and that would be the end of that. Isn't that the way young people were nowadays? They draw you into their lives and immerse you into their problems; then, just when you feel that you know them, they whip the rug right out from under you by doing something totally out of character. Or else they simply leave and you never hear from them again.

Esther pressed her hand against her forehead. Now who was she really thinking about here? Christine or her own daughter, Lenore? And why was she getting so confused? Perhaps Felicity was right. Perhaps she was getting a bit senile, or maybe it was even the onset of Alzheimer's. Good grief, she hoped not. She'd watched her best friend Barbara Winfield deteriorate from that dreadful disease until they'd finally put her in an awful nursing home. Esther had gone to visit a couple of times, but her friend had never recognized her, and after a while she'd quit going altogether. It had been something of a relief to everyone when the poor woman finally passed away. Esther would rather take a bottle of pills than end up like that. No, certainly, this wasn't Alzheimer's.

Maybe it was simply that Christine was about the same age Lenore had been.

Oh, she knew Christine was a year older and probably much more mature, but she still looked young. She had that youthful innocence about her. Not so unlike Lenore back before she went away. Esther sighed. For so many years she'd tried not to think about Lenore. She'd trained her mind to move on quickly whenever a memory sneaked in uninvited. She'd become an expert at distracting herself from thinking about the things that hurt.

But being laid up like this, with too much time and emptiness on her hands, made it more difficult than ever. Or maybe it was Christine's fault. Perhaps it was the presence of that silly girl that had placed Lenore on Esther's mind more than ever lately. But, in all fairness, she'd been thinking about her missing daughter even before she'd slipped and ruined her ankle. Perhaps that was even what had caused her to fall. Perhaps she hadn't been paying attention. Her mind might've been wandering down memory lane, wondering about all the what-ifs and whys about their lives, and as a result she'd stumbled. Who knew?

She'd confessed her troubles to her psychologist friend, May Ferrer, a couple months earlier. May had told her that it was only because she was growing older and naturally regretting some of her choices in life. And maybe that was true. But there seemed to be little to be done about it now. She'd always thought Lenore would come back home one day. She'd been certain of it. Many times Esther had imagined her pretty brown-haired daughter standing at the front door, sad-eyed and repentant, saying that she was sorry, that she'd been wrong, asking for her mother and stepfather to forgive her and allow her to return to her home and make a fresh start. And, naturally, Esther would've taken her back—in a heartbeat. She would've completely forgiven her only daughter. Oh, perhaps she would've given her a stern lecture first, about how she'd made bad choices but how we can all learn from our mistakes . . . But Lenore could've returned to her home, attended college, and gotten on with her life. She'd be close to forty by now. Forty? It seemed impossible. Esther couldn't imagine her sweet young daughter being forty. But then Esther had been a young forty herself. She'd gotten pregnant for the first time when she was all of thirty-nine. Perhaps forty wasn't so old after all. Esther knew she'd be just as happy to see her daughter at forty as she would've been when she was still nineteen. She wondered if Lenore had finished her schooling. Had she married? Were there children?

She'd always figured Lenore had the kind of beauty and intelligence to marry quite well. Esther had, in fact, already been scouting out available young men in the local community when Lenore was only eighteen. Not that she'd wanted her to marry young, but there seemed no harm in looking. And, naturally, she'd always considered those well-bred young men, always the sons of her closest friends, and coming from families of influence. In the early years, back when she expected her daughter to come home like a prodigal, she'd imagined the sort of wedding she'd give her. Something quiet and discreet, but certainly elegant. Perhaps with a reception in the backyard with a small orchestra from the music department. Oh, she knew Lenore wouldn't have been able to wear white. No sense being hypocrites. But then Lenore had always looked good in ecru. Esther had always imagined her lovely daughter going down the aisle in a beautiful lace gown of ecru.

She felt tears rolling down her cheeks and scolded herself for allowing her mind to run away with her. Goodness, she knew better than to dwell on Lenore like this. It only broke her heart. Again and again and again. Oh, why hadn't that foolish girl come home? Why had she been so stubborn? Why had she stayed away so long? Never called, never written, never looked back? How could anyone be so cruel and coldhearted?

9

It was after ten that night when Christine returned to her dorm. She'd never been a girl to be easily spooked, but after walking across the silent, empty campus, and then hearing the sound of her footsteps echoing down the hallway of the mostly vacant dorm, she suddenly imagined herself being followed, envisioned someone breaking into her room.

"Stop it!" she chided herself as she locked and deadbolted the door to her room behind her. She knew she was being ridiculous. But still the idea of spending the holidays alone in the dorm did feel a bit daunting just now. Of course, she had her grandmother's holiday party to plan and possibly, if she were lucky, to attend. Although she shouldn't assume too much. For all they knew she was simply the hired help. Certainly, they'd expect her to make herself scarce when it was actually time to celebrate Christmas. After all, she had no doubts that people like her grandmother and Felicity weren't the sort to invite the housekeeper to a social event. Of course, tonight had been an exception since the old woman had needed a ride. And even then Christine had mostly felt on the outside of things. Of course, she'd enjoyed the children and felt a real connection with them. But that would probably be a one-time thing.

That is, unless she decided to end this game of deception and break the news to her grandmother. Grandmother. It still sounded so foreign and unbelievable. She couldn't even believe she'd already been using that title for the cranky old woman. Especially since the only grandmother she'd previously known was her father's mother. Talk about your opposites. That grandmother had been tiny and soft-spoken, with curly white hair and soft, rosy cheeks. But she'd died a few years ago at the age of eighty-seven. But besides the physical differences, this grandmother hardly seemed like a grandmother at all. Not even to her two sweet little grandchildren. Even if they were her stepson's children, they seemed to have accepted her as their own.

But that was all beside the point, she told herself as she hurriedly prepared for bed. The dorm was colder than usual, and she'd been bundling up at night to stay warm. She layered on flannel pajamas, fuzzy socks, sweats, and even a knitted hat. The point was, she reminded herself, that she was suffering from a terribly guilty conscience for the way she was deceiving not only her grandmother but also her stepuncle, Jimmy, and his family. It was wrong, wrong, wrong, and she knew it. Even more than that, she knew she hadn't been brought up this way. And she knew her father would be disappointed in her. But perhaps worse than that, she knew God expected more from her too. Like honesty. As a result of all this guilt, she'd had difficulty praying this past week. And that was starting to take its toll on her in many ways. She felt more stressed and worried than ever, and she was actually starting to feel somewhat depressed too. And that was completely unlike her.

Tears of frustration began spilling down her cheeks, and she knew she had to make this right somehow. But that would mean blowing her cover and revealing her true identity. And she just wasn't sure she could do that. Not without risking everything. And, for some reason, it seemed more important than ever to find out about her birth mother and her family before they threw her out on her ear for tricking them. This need to know made her feel that no sacrifice would be too much.

She wished she could pray about it, to lay it all out there and simply ask God to help her, but she knew that was wrong. You can't very well ask God to help you deceive someone. Finally she settled for a quick "I'm sorry" and "Please help me" kind of prayer. It wasn't much, but it was more than she'd managed all week. And at least it was honest, or sort of honest. Maybe she'd wake up in the morning and everything would make sense again. And she'd know the perfect way to clear up this little misunderstanding. And everyone would be perfectly fine and happy. At least that's what she tried to make herself believe as she fell asleep.

As she walked to her grandmother's home the following morning, she didn't feel so hopeful or confident.

The dense, wet fog seemed only to add to her feelings of heaviness and gloom. At least Saturday was supposed to be a half day for her, and then she had Sunday off. And so she firmly told herself, *You have until noon to figure a way to tell your grandmother the truth.*

But by eleven thirty, the opportunity still hadn't arisen. Or perhaps she'd missed it completely. It didn't help matters that her grandmother had been in a foul mood all morning. Christine wasn't sure if this was because of the impending unwanted Christmas party or simply a result of being laid up with a bum ankle. Even so, Christine did her best to make the old woman comfortable and happy, but nothing seemed to help.

"My coffee is cold," her grandmother complained.

Christine considered telling her that it was cold because it had been sitting there too long, but she held her tongue. "I'll get you some more."

"Make it a fresh pot. I don't want any stale stuff."

So Christine made a fresh pot. But on the morning went, and nothing seemed to satisfy this cantankerous old woman. By the time it was noon and Christine had set a nice lunch tray next to her grandmother, she was emotionally exhausted.

"I put some dinner things on the shelf in the fridge," she said as she slipped on her parka. "Can I get you anything else?"

"No. I'm fine."

Christine frowned. "And you're sure you don't need me to come by tomorrow? I could come after church, you know."

"Jimmy promised to come by." She didn't even look up

from her soup. "I'll be fine. I'm not a baby, you know. I can do some things for myself."

Christine nodded. "Right. Well, you have the number to my dorm room if you should change your mind."

"I won't."

Christine walked slowly across campus. She wondered if she'd done something to upset her grandmother. She knew the woman wasn't the most congenial person, but it had seemed, up until today, that they'd been getting closer. She'd actually thought her grandmother liked her, at least a little bit. Or maybe she just tolerated her better than back in the beginning. But today had felt like a real setback. And Christine felt more frustrated and disappointed than ever. She'd wanted to sit down with the old woman, to look her right in the eyes and explain everything today. But there just never seemed an appropriate moment. And as grumpy as her grandmother was, she probably would've reacted quite badly. She most likely would've been seriously angry to hear the truth. Who knows, it might've totally ruined all possibilities of a relationship at all.

"What possibilities?" she had to ask herself as she crossed the street toward the dorm. When her grandmother found out she'd been deceived, she'd probably throw Christine out on the streets. And who could blame her? Maybe Christine should put the whole thing off until after Christmas. Perhaps that would be the kindest thing to do. Why should she risk upsetting the entire family?

Yes, she would wait until after the Christmas Eve party. Of course, that meant four more days of continuing this charade. But if Felicity was anything like Christine suspected, those would be four very busy and demanding days. Perhaps it was just as well that she was getting Sunday off. She felt fairly sure she'd need a day of rest just to prepare herself for all the work and preparation, not to mention the continued playacting, that was coming.

When Christine reported for work on Monday morning, she quickly discovered that Felicity had already made a complete list of things for her to do.

"Jimmy brought it by yesterday," her grandmother announced. "I hope you know what you've gotten yourself in for, young lady."

She glanced at the list, then smiled, purely for her grandmother's sake. "No problem. I can handle this," she said.

The old woman's brows lifted. "And keep up the quality of work you've been doing for me as well?"

She nodded. "You'll see."

Her grandmother rolled her eyes. "Yes, I suppose I will."

After lunch they sat down together to work on the computer. "I want you to show me how to search for a person," her grandmother said.

"There are a lot of ways," Christine explained. "First we choose a search engine."

"What?"

"Oh, it's like a service that works as a directory. Here, let me show you." She went to her favorite search site and pointed out the empty box. "We'll start by putting the name of the person in here and see if it pulls anything up. Is this person living or dead?"

"Living."

"Okay. Go ahead and type in the full name, and then we'll hit enter and see what comes up."

Christine stepped back and waited as her grandmother began to type. But she felt herself take in a fast breath when she saw the name. *Lenore Louise Blackstone.* In that same instant her stomach tied itself in a knot and her hands began to tremble.

"Okay, now what?"

Christine's mouth felt too dry to speak. And even if it hadn't, she still had no idea what to say. She felt slightly faint. She sat down on the chair across from the couch and took a deep breath, trying to regain some sense of composure.

"What's wrong?" her grandmother asked as she looked over at Christine. "Goodness, you look pale. Aren't you feeling well?"

Christine shook her head.

"Good grief, I hope you haven't picked up that horrible flu bug. That's all I need right now. Maybe you'd better run along home until you know what it is that's ailing you. I certainly can't afford to get that flu with my ankle still bummed up. I can barely get around as it is. That would land me in the hospital for certain. I mean it, Christine, you'd better get out of here right now."

Christine stood up and walked to the closet, retrieved her parka, and left. She knew it was stupid. She didn't have the flu. But, at the same time, she didn't know if she could tell her grandmother the truth right now.

"Oh, what tangled webs we weave . . . ," she said to herself as she started heading back toward her dorm. Then, instead of going to her dorm, she decided to stop by her church. It was only a few blocks out of the way, and she hoped she might be able to get a word with the pastor. She felt she was in deep need of some wise counsel. How had she gotten herself into this mess, anyway? By lying, of course. That was simple enough. But now she needed to find a way to get out.

"What brings you here?" Pastor Reinhart asked. "Coming to complain about yesterday's sermon?"

She shook her head. "Actually, I just needed someone to talk to."

His brow creased. "Have a chair. Is everything okay with your father? I hear bits and pieces of news about South America, but, to be honest, I don't pay that much attention. Everything going all right down there?"

She nodded. "That's not what's troubling me."

He sat down behind his desk, then leaned forward. "Well, that's a relief. So, tell me, what's making you look so glum?"

She poured out her story, and he listened, making careful comments here and there, until she was completely finished.

"Wow. That's quite a story," he said. "I know of the Daniels family. James Daniels used to be the president of the university. Quite a powerful and respected man in the community. He passed away a few years ago. They had a big memorial service."

She nodded.

"I've never met Mrs. Daniels, but I know she used to be quite involved in community affairs. Her name would appear in the paper quite frequently."

She nodded again.

"Of course, that's not what you came to talk about. Is it?"

"What should I do now?" she implored. "I need help."

He pressed his lips together. "Well . . . I think you know what you need to do, Christine."

"I know."

"And, the way I see it, the sooner is usually the better. Lies don't get smaller over time. You can sweep them under the rug, but they won't stay there for long."

"Do you think she'll be mad?"

He shrugged. "It's hard to say. I'm sure she's a fairly proud woman, and most people don't like being deceived."

"That's true."

"But, on the other hand, she should be happy to learn that she has a granddaughter." He smiled warmly. "Especially someone like you, Christine. Did I tell you that Beth Maxwell said you did an absolutely brilliant job with her third graders while she was on vacation last month? She thinks you should take a class of your own whenever one opens up."

Christine smiled weakly.

"I know. I know. That's not what you need to hear right now." He folded his hands. "Sometimes the truth is hard to hear, but I think you knew it before you came in here."

Christine looked down at her lap. "What about her daughter, Pastor Reinhart? I mean my mother . . . My grandmother doesn't even know Lenore is dead."

"Unfortunately, you're going to have to tell her." He shook his head. "It's very sad. But you need to remember that it's not your fault. You're just the messenger."

"The messenger who messed up."

He chuckled. "Well, it'll probably smooth out. Just go and tell her the truth. I can tell it's eating you up inside. You don't need that, especially at Christmastime. Besides, I have a feeling it's all going to work out just fine. I think your grandmother is going to be really happy to realize she's got a granddaughter."

"Do you think we could really have a relationship like that?" She stood and made her way to the door, as she realized her pastor must have other things to do. "Do you think that's really possible?"

"All things are possible with God. Just put it in his hands."

As she walked back toward the Daniels home, she did just that. She put the whole thing into God's hands.

When she rang the doorbell to the house, she felt stronger and braver than she'd felt in days. That is, until she saw her grandmother's face.

"What on earth are you doing back here?" she demanded. "I thought you were sick."

"We need to talk," Christine said in a sober voice.

10

Christine prayed silently as she followed her grandmother into the living room. It seemed the old woman was maneuvering her crutches much better these days. Perhaps her ankle was improving and she wasn't in such pain. Maybe it wouldn't be long before she didn't need Christine's help anymore. Christine noticed a dust bunny she'd missed beneath the table in the hallway. She'd have to go over the hardwood floors more carefully later. It was surprising how familiar this home had become to her during the past week. Like she'd known it for years.

"So you don't have the flu after all?" her grandmother asked as she eased herself into the recliner and frowned at Christine. "What is it then?"

Christine sighed and then looked down at her lap.

"Oh, no," her grandmother exclaimed in a horrified voice.

Christine quickly looked up. "What?"

"Don't tell me you've gone and gotten yourself pregnant. And you, supposedly a good church girl."

Christine shook her head. "That's not it."

"Well." Her grandmother leaned back. "That's a relief."

Christine took a deep breath. "This is rather hard to explain."

Her grandmother frowned. "What is it? Are you in some kind of trouble with the law?"

"No. That's not it. But I do have something to tell you that might not be easy to hear."

"What is it?" she demanded.

"Well, it's hard to know the best way to begin . . ."

"Just tell me." She leaned forward and peered at Christine. "At once!"

"All right," Christine said. "But you better brace yourself."

"I am losing my patience!"

"Okay." Christine winced, then quickly said it. "I'm Lenore Blackstone's daughter."

The room grew so silent that Christine could hear her grandmother's breathing coming out in short, ragged puffs. She stared at the stunned woman sitting across from her, watching with fear as the color drained from her grandmother's face. What if she suffered a stroke or heart attack from the shock? Why hadn't Christine thought this through better? Broken it to her more carefully?

"Are you okay?" Christine asked.

Her grandmother said nothing. Just sat there and stared as if seeing a ghost.

"I'm so sorry to tell you like this," Christine said. "I came here originally with the intent of introducing myself to you, but then you assumed I was here for the job, and you just kept talking to me like I was having an interview, and, well, I was so nervous and scared that I just went along with it, and I meant to tell you the next day, but then I got caught up in the job and in helping you, and the more time went on, the harder it became to tell you—"

"Silence!"

Christine blinked, then leaned back into the couch. "Sorry . . . ," she muttered.

Her grandmother shook her head sharply, as if she was trying to shake some sense out of what she'd just heard. "Are you actually telling me that Lenore Blackstone, my only daughter, is your mother?"

Christine nodded.

"My daughter is your mother?" she said it slowly this time, as if it were still sinking in.

"My *birth* mother." Christine added. She still thought of Marie Bradley as her real mother. Lenore was little more than a stranger to her. "My parents adopted me at birth."

"And that would've been about twenty years ago?" Her grandmother seemed to be doing some math in her head. "The same year she left home?"

"I guess so."

Her grandmother sighed. "She was pregnant with you when she left."

"That's what I'd heard."

Suddenly her grandmother sat up straight and eagerly looked at Christine with what seemed like an almost child-like hope and expectancy. "So, tell me, do you know anything about Lenore now? Do you know where she lives or whether she's married or has other children? Can you give me her address?"

Christine felt a lump growing in her throat. "I'm—I'm sorry," she began, then choked on the words. "But sh—she's dead."

Her grandmother sank back into her chair like she'd been deflated. She leaned her head back, then closed her eyes and moaned as if she were in great pain.

Christine, worried for the old woman's health, jumped up and went to her side. "Are you okay?"

"Oh no. Oh no. Oh no," she muttered in an almost incoherent way.

"Shall I call someone?" Christine asked. "Do you need help?"

Her grandmother slowly shook her head, eyes still closed, still moaning. Christine wasn't sure what to do now. Was this turning into a medical emergency? Should she call Jimmy and Felicity? She put her hand on her grandmother's shoulder and silently prayed for help and guidance. She begged God to comfort this poor woman in the grief she'd so carelessly poured upon her.

"I'm sorry to be the one to tell you about Lenore," Christine said. "I thought you already knew, but then you wanted to look her up on the computer and I realized—"

"When did she die?" her grandmother said suddenly. She sat up and looked at Christine. "And why wasn't I notified?"

"My parents tried to find you, but they didn't know your name was Daniels back then. Apparently, they attempted to locate a Mr. and Mrs. Blackstone in this town but couldn't. Lenore died nearly twenty years ago, just a month after I was born. She was hit by a car. Since my parents were unable to reach any of her relatives, they just handled the funeral arrangements and everything themselves. They'd been good friends to Lenore. She'd even been living with them for a while. That's about all I know."

"Is there a gravesite?" she asked in a hollow voice.

"Yes, it's in Larchwood, my hometown."

"I'd like to see it."

Christine nodded. "I know where it is. I've been there a few times, and my mother's grave is nearby. I can take you there if you think you're up to it."

She shook her head. "Not today. I don't think I can handle much more today." Then she looked at Christine and frowned. "You were dishonest with me."

"I know. And I'm really sorry." Christine sat back down on the couch, preparing herself for her grandmother's chastening.

"I don't like being tricked by anyone, young lady, even if it is my own granddaughter." She narrowed her eyes. "In fact . . . why should I even believe you now? Perhaps you're *not* my granddaughter. Perhaps you've made all this up, and maybe Lenore is still alive. How do I know you're not lying to me right now?"

Christine considered this. "Why would I do that?"

"Well, you admit to lying to me before, right?"

"Not outright lying," Christine said. "But I guess I didn't tell you the complete truth."

"So how do I know you're not lying now?"

Christine felt confused. "But what reason would I have to lie about something like this?"

"Money." She studied Christine carefully, almost as if she were examining a bug beneath a magnifying glass. "You could be here to scam an old woman into giving you some kind of inheritance." Then she laughed, but it was that old cynical, menacing laugh again. "That is, assuming this old woman has anything to leave anyone. And that's a pretty big assumption."

Christine shook her head. "No, I don't want your money. I only wanted—"

"Well, of course you wouldn't admit to wanting my money. What kind of scam artist would do something as stupid as that? No, you're a clever girl, Christine. First you'd ingratiate yourself to me and to my family. Then you'd reveal your identity, and then you'd wait around for the money."

Christine stood up. "That's not true."

"How do I know what's true and what's not? Everything you've done up until now has been a big, fat lie. Why should I believe anything you have to say?"

Christine felt hot tears burning in her eyes. Tears of anger and indignation. "I'm telling you the truth," she said. "I have absolutely no reason to lie."

"How can I know?"

Tears were streaming down Christine's face now. "Look, I'm sorry I deceived you before. That was stupid and wrong and thoughtless. But I am telling you the truth now. I am Lenore Blackstone's daughter. You can call my father and ask him." She rushed over to the desk and wrote down the phone number of the mission compound in Brazil.

"Call him if you don't believe me." Then she turned and ran out the front door and away from the house.

She cried as she walked back to the dorm. Why had she been such an idiot? Why hadn't she just told the truth from the beginning? She wished she could turn back the clock. But if she could, she wouldn't bother going back over the past couple of weeks. Instead she'd turn the clock back to at least six years ago. Back to when both her parents were alive and well. And they were all together and happily enjoying the Christmas holidays the way they were meant to be enjoyed. With warmth and love and family. Something she'd taken so for granted at the time, but something that might never happen again.

11

Christine awoke to the shrill sound of the phone ringing. She reached for the phone, fumbling in the darkness to find it. "Hello?"

"Christine?" It was a male voice but not her father's.

"Yes." She flipped on the light and glanced at the clock. It was only eight thirty, but it felt more like midnight. How long had she been sleeping?

"This is Jimmy. I'm sorry to disturb you, but my mother called a bit ago. And she was very upset and actually sounded a little bit delirious—"

"Is she okay?" Christine asked.

"I think so. Felicity just gave her a pain pill and helped her to bed, but we're feeling concerned . . ." He cleared his throat. "She said some strange things about you. I don't know if she's imagining things or—"

"Did she mention Lenore?"

"Yes. First she said that Lenore was dead, and then she

102

said that it was all just a lie and that you were not to be trusted."

Christine sighed. "It's a long story."

"I've got time."

So Christine attempted to explain it all to him, carefully going over the details she knew, and how she'd never meant to trick his mother, and how she was very sorry. "And you can call my father down in Brazil to verify everything. I'm sure this information must all be on my birth certificate, which I think must be in his safety deposit box at the bank. In fact, I have a key, if it would help matters to see it."

"Oh, I don't think that's necessary, Christine. I believe you, myself. I mean, why would you make something like this up?"

"Your mother thought I might be a scam artist trying to con her out of her money."

He laughed. "Yeah, that sounds like something she might say. But don't worry. The truth is you remind me a little bit of Lenore." He grew quieter. "I'm really sad to hear that she's dead. But I'd wondered about that possibility. She just didn't seem like the kind of person who would leave like that and never come back or call or anything. She always seemed a very kind and forgiving person to me."

"That's nice to know," Christine said. "Actually, the main reason I wanted to contact Lenore's family was to learn more about her."

"I didn't know her really well," he explained. "I was already in college when our parents got married, and that was only a few years before Lenore, uh, left."

"Did you know she was pregnant when she left home?"

"I suspected as much. I think it was supposed to be some big secret, but it wasn't hard to guess what was going on."

"Is there anything I can do to help your mother?" she asked. "I wasn't sure whether I should come back and work for her after this. I mean, she was pretty upset with me."

"Well, that's the problem. You see, Aunt Hattie is supposed to arrive tomorrow. And Felicity has her hands full trying to get things ready for Christmas. And we could use your help, if you don't mind, that is."

"I don't mind at all. I just don't want to upset your mother by being around."

"How about this?" he said. "What if I pick you up tomorrow and bring you back over to Mom's, and the three of us can sit and talk this thing out?"

Christine sighed in relief. "Would you?"

"Hey, I'd be happy to. After all, you're family."

She smiled. "I guess you're sort of like my uncle, then. Although I realize you're really a stepuncle."

"Hey, you can call me Uncle Jimmy anytime you like. Suits me just fine."

"Thanks. And thanks for calling. I feel a lot better now."

"See you around eight in the morning, then?"

"Sounds great."

Christine prayed for her grandmother before she went back to bed that night. She asked God to help her adjust to the hard news of losing her only daughter. And then she asked him to help her forgive her granddaughter for lying.

Esther awoke in the darkness with an overwhelming feeling of confusion and sadness. *What's wrong with me?*

she wondered as she reached to turn on the lamp on her bedside table. Then she remembered. Lenore. Lenore was dead. Or so said that manipulative girl who had tricked her way into Esther's life and home. She should've known better. If it sounds too good to be true . . .

She swung her legs over the side of the bed, cautiously extending her injured foot lest she bump it against the side rail again. She'd done that enough times to remember to be more careful. Then she frowned as she noticed that her crutches, instead of being right next to her bed where they should've been, were clear across the room.

"That silly Felicity," she muttered as she slowly worked her way to the foot of the bed and then used the bench as a very short walker to enable her to finally reach her crutches. Then, with her crutches beneath her, and nearly out of breath, she managed to locate her robe and slippers. Not thoughtfully laid out like when that girl had been working here. She no longer thought of Christine by name. Instead she had become *that girl* in her mind. That evil, deceptive, selfish, lying girl.

"Can't believe I was such a fool as to be duped like that," she mumbled as she slowly made her way down the hall toward the living room. She knew she wasn't going to be able to fall asleep again. She'd hoped she might be able to simply sit and relax in her recliner, preferably with a hot cup of tea, but that was probably too much to attempt on her own tonight. She'd have to settle for the comfort of the recliner. But before she reached the recliner, she paused at her desk, noticing the writing scrawled across the notepad. "Allen Bradley, CMA compound," followed by a long phone number that appeared to be international.

Although that could have just as well been made up too. That girl probably didn't think Esther would call her bluff. But then she just didn't know what a tough broad she was up against either.

Esther sat down at her desk and picked up the phone. But then she looked at the clock. It was a little past three in the morning and probably not the best hour to be dialing what was most likely a wrong number. No sense in disturbing innocent people. She glanced down at the bottom drawer, then shook her head. "It's not true, Esther," she told herself. "It's all a big, fat lie. That girl is just trying to pull one over on you. Don't fall for her tricks."

The contents of the drawer seemed to be pulling her hand down toward it as if it had a magnetic force of its own. Finally she gave in and leaned down and tugged on the stubborn drawer. Once it was open, she slowly reached inside, removed the framed photo, then turned it over to stare at the lovely young woman who seemed to have been captured in time. She sat for a long time just staring at the image of her daughter. She hadn't even noticed the tears that had fallen from her eyes and splattered like raindrops on the glass surface covering the photo. She used the sleeve of her robe to wipe it clean, rubbing it over and over in circles as if to polish it.

"Lenore," she whispered. "Tell me it's not true." But even as she said these words, she knew that it was indeed true. She knew beyond any shadow of doubt that Lenore was dead. Dead and gone and buried just like that girl had said. It was the eyes that told her so. Those big, golden-brown eyes that had the fresh look of youth and innocence, and honesty, in them. The same eyes that Lenore had passed down to her daughter, Christine.

Esther set Lenore's picture on her desk and faced it toward the recliner. Then she slowly made her way across the room and eased herself into the recliner. And there she sat, gazing at the photo through her tears, wishing desperately that she could do it all differently.

12

Christine sat on the cement steps in front of her dorm as she waited for Jimmy to pick her up. As she sat she prayed that God would do something miraculous to salvage the mess she'd created. *I'm sorry that I didn't tell the truth from the beginning. But I do believe you can take our worst failures and turn them into your successes. That's all I'm asking you to do. Just bring something good out of this for my grandmother. Help her through this sadness, and heal her wounded heart.*

Just then she saw the Ford Explorer pull up with Jimmy waving from inside. "Hey," he called as he stuck his head out the window. "Am I late?"

She jogged up to the SUV. "No. I was just early."

"How you doing?" he asked as she buckled her seat belt.

"Okay, I guess. Considering." She sighed. "But I really do feel bad for making such a mess of everything for your stepmother."

"*Your* grandmother."

She nodded. "Yeah. But I doubt she'll ever want me to call her that. In fact, I won't be surprised if she refuses to let me into her house. She was really mad at me yesterday."

"I know. But she can be like that. She might come across as pretty feisty and mean, but underneath everything she has a very tender heart."

Christine studied him in wonder. Of all the members of the Daniels family, Jimmy seemed the most thoughtful and kind. "Can I ask you a question, Jimmy?"

"Sure."

"What makes you so nice?"

He laughed. "Oh, you should see me getting down on the boys' basketball team lately. I'm sure they wouldn't agree with that assessment."

"Well, I appreciate your help in this."

"Hey, we're family now. And I happen to think Mom needs someone like you around right now."

"It's interesting that you call her Mom. I mean, she's really your stepmom, and she's not always exactly nice to you."

He smiled. "Well, she and I have an understanding. Both my parents have passed on, and she's always been there for me. I guess I've pretty much adopted her as *Mom*."

"That's cool."

"Sometimes family isn't so much about whose DNA you're carrying as it is about love. You know?"

"Definitely. I mean, my parents aren't my birth parents, but I love them both more than anything."

"Even so, I think it's important that you get involved in Mom's life. Like I said before, I think she needs you."

"Even after the way I deceived her?"

"Hey, we all make mistakes, Christine. It's the way we deal with them afterward that makes a difference."

"Yeah, I'm sure you're right. But I usually don't make mistakes of this caliber."

"Well, if it makes you feel any better, I can understand how this whole thing might've happened. I know as well as anyone that Mom can be pretty intimidating, and if she gets going in a certain direction, it can be awfully hard to derail her. Besides that, you've been an excellent caregiver to her. That's something."

"I actually really like her. Although I wasn't too sure at first. I mean, she can be, well, like you said, intimidating."

He laughed. "Yeah, and I can think of a few other words people might use to describe her. But they're not very nice words."

"Can I ask you something else?"

"Shoot."

"What's up with her and your Aunt Hattie?"

He blew a long, low whistle. "Funny you should ask . . . since that's a can of worms that has just turned potentially explosive." He laughed. "Wow, talk about mixing your metaphors. You can sure tell I don't teach English."

"What do you mean by explosive?"

"Well, now that Mom knows Lenore is dead, and Aunt Hattie is here . . . Well, it might get interesting or ugly, or who knows . . . maybe they'll fall into each other's arms and forgive each other for everything. Now, wouldn't that be something." He pulled into the driveway.

"But what does Aunt Hattie have to do with Lenore?" Christine asked, eager to get to the bottom of this before they went inside.

"I don't know the full story. I don't think anyone really does. Well, besides Aunt Hattie and Mom, that is. But they got into it at Dad's funeral. All I know is that it had to do with Dad and Lenore and there was a lot of blame and accusation going on. But I never heard exactly why or what, which was probably just as well. But, as you could tell the other night, Mom is still not over it. And I'm not too sure about Aunt Hattie either." He turned off the ignition and got out of the SUV. "Although Aunt Hattie never brings it up, not to me anyway. In fact, she acts as if nothing ever happened. But then she's a sweet little lady. I'm hoping she plans to help Mom to bury the hatchet."

"That'd be good."

"You're going to like Aunt Hattie, Christine. She and Mom are complete opposites." He laughed as they walked up to the front door. "Being so different makes me think these two old gals should actually get along better."

Christine's heart was pounding like a jackhammer as she followed Jimmy down the hallway. Was she making a mistake in coming back here so soon? Perhaps Esther needed more time to recover from her shock.

"Mom," he called in a cheerful voice as they approached her bedroom. "You up yet?"

But her bed was empty. It looked as if there had been some sort of struggle, with the satin comforter half on the floor and the bench overturned against the wall.

"Goodness," Christine said. "I hope she's okay."

They hurried out to the living room to discover her asleep in her recliner, snoring softly.

"She looks fine to me," he whispered to Christine.

"What?" Esther jerked herself awake. "Who is it? What's going on?"

"Hi, Mom," Jimmy said, walking over to her chair. "It's just me, coming to check on you. I brought Christine with me, and before you get yourself all riled up, we'd like to sit down and talk to you, rationally."

She nodded without saying anything.

Jimmy pointed to the couch. "Take a seat, Christine."

She followed his order and sat down across from her grandmother. Then she waited as he pulled up a side chair and sat next to his stepmom. The three of them sat in a triangle, and Jimmy began to speak. "I know that you think Christine is lying about Lenore, but I've talked with her and gone over some things, and I have no reason to think she's not telling the truth." He held up one finger. "For one thing, she can produce a birth certificate from her dad's safety deposit box." He held up two fingers. "And she said you can call her dad and ask him." He put up a third finger. "And she can take you to Lenore's grave and—"

"That's enough, Jimmy," she snapped. "No more fingers."

"But, Mom."

"And no more buts." She glanced at Christine and then back to Jimmy. "I know she's Lenore's daughter. I think that, somewhere inside of me, I knew it from the very first day she showed up at my door." She looked down in her lap and let out a long sigh. "And I also know that Lenore's dead. The truth is I think I've known it all along. I just never wanted to admit it before."

"I wish I'd been bringing you happier news," Christine said.

"Well, it doesn't do any good to beat up the messenger," Jimmy said.

"I'm so sorry about everything," Christine told her grandmother. "I hope someday you'll be able to forgive me. But I'll understand if you don't."

"Don't call me Esther anymore," she said.

Christine nodded, feeling certain that she was about to be dismissed for good.

"You can call me Grandmother," she continued. "Or Grandma, I suppose, like Jimmy's kids do. Although I'm not particularly fond of that title." Her lips turned up at the edges just slightly. "And I'm sorry I didn't believe you yesterday, Christine. I guess I just hoped it wasn't true, about Lenore, I mean. No one likes to learn that their child has . . . has died . . ."

"I'm so sorry," Christine said, wishing she could say something else. But nothing else seemed to work.

Her grandmother slowly shook her head. "There should be a law . . . ," she said in a tired voice. "There should be a law that children should never die before their parents do—" She began to choke up again. "But I guess I'm partly to blame for Lenore's death. I—I never should've—" She put her hands over her face and began to sob.

"Oh, Mom," Jimmy said, reaching over to put his hand on her heaving shoulders. "You can't go blaming yourself for Lenore's death."

Christine wasn't sure she could watch this display of emotion without falling apart herself. She felt she was barely holding it together as it was, and so she excused herself and headed off to the kitchen to make some strong coffee and fix breakfast just the way Esther—just the way *Grandmother*—liked it.

Her grandmother seemed nearly recovered when Christine appeared with the breakfast tray. "You should probably eat something," she told her as she set the tray on the table next to her.

"Good thinking," Jimmy said. "Sorry to run off like this, but I promised Felicity I'd watch the kids while she does some quick Christmas shopping. And, by the way, she'll be picking up Aunt Hattie at the train station."

"Speaking of Aunt Hattie," Esther said. "I wonder if Felicity couldn't keep her for a while today." She glanced at Christine. "We have something we need to attend to, if that's okay with you, Christine."

She shrugged. "I'm at your disposal, Grandmother."

Esther smiled. "Good."

"I'm sure that'll be okay with Felicity," Jimmy assured them. "Maybe we could take the old girl out for an early dinner tonight. I wonder if she still likes Chinese food."

"I wouldn't know," Esther said stiffly.

Christine wished she could ask her grandmother about the conflict between her and her sister-in-law, but in light of all the recent emotional upheavals, she felt it unwise.

"Then we can drop Aunt Hattie by the house this evening?" Jimmy asked.

Esther nodded with a grim expression. "That should be fine."

After breakfast Christine helped her grandmother bathe and dress as usual, but perhaps with just a bit more tenderness than before. She didn't say much.

"You're being awfully quiet," her grandmother said as Christine helped her slip her good foot into a loafer.

"Sorry."

"I would think you'd be filled with questions."

Christine looked up at her. "Oh, I am. But I hate to push things too much. You've had a lot to take in. I guess we both have."

She nodded. "You're pretty wise for your age. Well, in most things. I still don't think it was terribly wise to trick me like that. But then I suppose it seemed right at the time."

"What is it we need to take care of today?" Christine asked. "I suppose we need to pick up a few more groceries since we're having company . . ."

"Yes, there's that too. But first we need to drive over to Larchwood."

Christine nodded. "To see her grave."

"Yes. I need to do that."

"Do you want to stop by the bank and see my birth certificate too?" Christine asked.

Esther shook her head. "No, I don't think that's necessary."

"I do have a question that's pestered me more than most," Christine said as she drove toward Larchwood. "It's about my birth father."

Esther looked out the passenger window without answering.

"But it's okay if you'd rather not talk about it now," she said quickly. "I'm just curious, you know."

"The problem is that I'm not too sure, Christine. At the

time I really thought it was Lenore's on-again, off-again boyfriend, Peter Summers. I never really approved of the young man and didn't feel he was a good match for Lenore. But when I bumped into him on campus one day, just a few months after she'd left, I confronted him about the pregnancy, and he completely denied everything. Of course, Lenore had insisted from the very beginning that it wasn't Peter's child." Esther turned and looked out the window again. "But I didn't listen."

"Do you have any idea who my father might be?" Christine asked. She didn't like the idea that her birth mother had possibly been the kind of girl to sleep around and not even know who the father of her child was. It didn't fit with the image Christine had built into her head. But then again if it was the truth, it would be best to just get it out in the open.

Without answering, her grandmother opened her Gucci handbag and reached in for a handkerchief to dab her eyes.

"I'm sorry if I'm upsetting you," Christine said. "We can talk about something else."

She nodded. "Yes, I think I'd appreciate that."

But they didn't talk about anything else. They just drove the next forty minutes in silence. But Christine knew what they were both thinking about, or rather whom. Lenore Blackstone was very much on their minds. As they entered Larchwood, Christine broke the silence. "The house I grew up in is down that street." She pointed toward Meadow Lane.

"Drive past it," Esther said.

Christine turned down the street and drove the five

blocks to her house. "That's it," she said as she parked on the other side of the street from the small clapboard-sided house. "It was always yellow when we lived there. That was my mother's favorite color. The new renters must've painted it." She felt a tightness in her chest, a longing to go back to her safe childhood world.

"It's awfully small," her grandmother said. "But I think it would've looked better painted yellow."

Christine smiled. "It did."

"And you lived there your whole life?"

She nodded.

"And is that the house where Lenore stayed with your parents?"

"Yes. My parents lived there for more than ten years before I was born. The mortgage is completely paid off, and the rent money is supporting my dad while he's volunteering in the mission school. It was his lifelong dream."

"Well, good for him. Your parents sound like fine people, Christine. I'm thankful for that. For your sake, I mean."

"So am I." Christine began to pull away, resisting the urge to look back. "It used to bother me some, as a child, that my parents were so much older than everyone else's. I guess I was actually embarrassed by them sometimes. I'm ashamed to think of that now."

"Kids always have problems with their parents," her grandmother said. "It's just the way of life."

"But these past couple of years I've really learned to appreciate all my parents have done for me. Unfortunately, it was too late to show it to my mother. But I try to let my dad know."

"I'm sure he knows, Christine. You know, I'd like to write

him a letter. To thank him for his kindness to my—my girls."

"Oh, he would love that, Grandmother. And you'll have to meet him when he comes back from Brazil. He's the sweetest person ever."

"Do you have any photos of your family?"

"I do. I even made up a little album last summer. I wish I had a photo of Lenore, but my dad said she was camera shy."

Esther nodded. "That's true, she was. A beautiful girl, but she hated getting her picture taken. So I don't have many photos of her after she became a teenager. I do have quite a few of her as a baby and young child. You can see them when we get back home."

They had reached the edge of town. "Shall I drive to the cemetery now? Or do you think we should stop and get something to eat? It's past lunchtime."

Esther waved her hand. "I'm perfectly fine. Why don't we just keep going. Those thick, gray clouds look like they might have snow in them."

"Oh, I hope so," Christine said. "I'd love to have a white Christmas this year."

Esther just shook her head.

When they reached the cemetery, Christine could feel a silence settling into the car, like a thick blanket of sadness draped around them. "Lenore's grave isn't too far from the road," she said, hoping to alleviate the heaviness. "It's near my mother's. I think you can make it there fairly easily with your crutches."

She parked the car as close as she could to the gravesite, then went around to help her grandmother out of the car.

The wind was biting cold, and Christine thought she saw a few snowflakes fluttering through the air.

"It's right next to this path," she said, pointing down the graveled walk. "But be careful with those crutches, this ground isn't terribly even." She stayed near the old woman, keeping her hands ready to support her if she stumbled. But soon they were there, and, thankfully, there was a marble bench directly across from Lenore's grave. It must've been placed there by the people who maintained a family plot just adjacent to hers, but the two of them sat down on it just the same.

Esther pulled her handkerchief from her pocket and dabbed at her eyes as she stared speechlessly at the small granite marker.

LENORE LOUISE BLACKSTONE
1965–1984
SAFE IN HER FATHER'S ARMS
JOHN 3:16

Christine sat in silence for several minutes, then finally said, "My dad told me Lenore had a really good heart, that she was kind and good and gentle. And I don't know if it'll make any difference to you. I mean, I don't know where you stand about these things, but my dad said Lenore gave her heart to God not long before she died. That's always been reassuring to me."

Esther turned away, holding her handkerchief over her face as she sobbed quietly. Christine laid a hand on her shoulder. "I know it's hard, Grandmother, but I really believe she's happy now."

Esther shook her head. "No, this is—all—all my fault. My daughter is dead and gone because I was so—so wrong. So stubborn and wrong." Suddenly she stood, clumsily gathering her crutches beneath her as she began moving closer to the grave. "Oh, Lenore," she sobbed. "I was so wrong—" And then, like a house of cards, she crumbled and fell on the dry brown grass.

"Grandmother!" Christine shrieked as she fell on her knees next to the old woman. "Are you okay?"

But her grandmother's eyes were closed, and though she was breathing, it was coming out in quick little pants. Christine gently shook her, then looked around to see if anyone was nearby. Oh, how she wished she had a cell phone just then.

"What's the problem?" a male voice called.

Christine whipped around to see a man in overalls and a sweatshirt jogging toward them. "It's my grandmother," she said. "She's collapsed. Please, can you call an ambulance?"

The man pulled some sort of radio from his pocket, telling someone on the other end to call for an ambulance. Then he knelt beside Esther and leaned over to see if she was breathing.

"She's still breathing," Christine said.

"Is it her heart?" he asked. "Does she need CPR?"

Christine had already checked her pulse. "She has a heartbeat, but it's not very strong. I'm not sure what to do."

"The ambulance should be here soon." The man whipped off his sweatshirt and used it to cradle Esther's head. "The hospital's only about a mile away."

"That's right," Christine remembered. Then she removed

120

her own parka and laid it over her grandmother to help preserve her body heat. In the same moment, as if to mock her, the snowflakes began to fall faster.

"Oh, hurry," she cried. "Please, please, hurry." Then she began to pray. *Dear God, please take care of Grandmother. Please help her to be all right. And please send the ambulance quickly.*

Just then she heard the siren coming closer. Within minutes the whole crew was there, checking her grandmother's vital signs, putting an oxygen mask on her, and loading her onto the gurney.

"I'll follow you," Christine said as she turned to run back to the car.

As she drove toward the hospital, she continued to pray. But as she parked the car and dashed toward the ER entrance, it hit her. This was where her mother had died only five years ago. And, most likely, though she'd never asked, this was where Lenore had died nearly twenty years ago. Would this be where her grandmother would die today?

Please, God, no, she prayed as she pushed open the doors.

"You'll have to wait out here," the receptionist said after Christine quickly explained the situation. "We'll let you know when Mrs. Daniels is stabilized, and then you can see her."

First Christine paced back and forth, and then it occurred to her that her grandmother had other family that should be notified. She ran to the pay phone and dialed information to get Jimmy and Felicity's number. Jimmy was supposed to be home with his kids today.

"Hello?" His voice sounded as cheerful as ever.

"Jimmy," she gasped. "This is Christine. I'm at the hospital in Larchwood with your mother—"

"Oh no, is she okay? What happened?"

Christine quickly told him about what had happened at the cemetery.

"I guess it was just too much for her." She was crying now. "I should've known better than to take her. But she seemed to be doing so well, and she really wanted to go. And then she just fell apart. Oh, it's all my fault—"

"Easy does it, girl. It's not your fault at all. It's just the way things go sometimes. And, knowing Mom, I'm guessing she's going to be just fine. That woman is really resilient. Just the same, I'll be over just as soon as I can. But I may have to bring the rugrats with me."

"That's okay. I can help watch them," she offered.

Then she went and sat down in a hard vinyl chair. She leaned over and put her head in her hands and just cried. Why did this keep happening to her? And just when she thought she'd gotten a grandmother, it looked like she might lose her. *Maybe it's me*, she thought. *Maybe I'm some kind of jinx to everyone I love or have any connections to. Maybe I should just wear a big caution sign across my chest, warning people to beware—don't get too close.* But, at the same time, she knew she was being ridiculous. Still, she couldn't help but wonder if she'd played the granddaughter-for-a-day game—and lost.

By the time Jimmy and the kids arrived, Christine still hadn't been told anything, and every time she inquired the receptionist grew more exasperated with her, telling her not to worry so much and that she just needed to be more patient. "These things take time."

"You'd think they could tell us *something*," she said to Jimmy. "I mean, is she okay? Was it a heart attack? A stroke? What? Even if we can't see her, they ought to know something by now." She glanced at her watch. "It's been well over an hour."

"Let me go give it a try," he said. "You kids stay with your cousin and I'll be back in a minute."

She smiled at that word. *Cousin*. It sounded comforting.

"Where's Grandma?" Jamie asked as he sat down beside Christine.

"She's in there." Christine pointed toward the big swinging doors. "The doctor is with her now."

"Is she getting a shot?" Casey asked with wide eyes. "I don't like getting shots."

"I don't know," Christine said honestly. "She might be getting a shot."

"We got our Christmas tree," Jamie said as he noticed a small artificial tree on the reception desk.

Casey clapped her hands. "Our tree is so big it touches the ceiling, and Daddy put an angel on top."

"It must be beautiful."

"And we have presents," Jamie said. "We even have one for you."

Christine blinked. "For me?"

He nodded. "Me and Daddy picked it out."

Suddenly she realized that she was part of the family now and that she still needed to get Christmas presents. However, that responsibility seemed to pale in comparison to today's medical emergency. "All things in due time," her father would probably tell her.

"I spoke to the doctor," Jimmy said. "She's okay."

"Really?" Christine wasn't sure whether she could believe this or not. "I mean, is she really okay okay? Or is she just stabilized? Was it her heart or—"

He held up his hand to stop her. "Let me tell you. They checked her heart and everything, and it all looks pretty good. The doctor says it was probably low blood sugar and exhaustion. I told him about visiting the grave, and he said that might've contributed to everything. But the good news is she's just fine."

"Thank God," Christine said as she sank down into a chair. "I thought for sure that I was going to lose her. I mean everyone was going to lose her. But it just didn't seem fair after getting to be her granddaughter for only a day."

He laughed. "Well, don't worry. It looks like the old girl will be around for a good long time. I'd better call Felicity though. I left a somewhat urgent message on her cell phone, and if she got it, she's probably coming a little unglued by now."

"Grandma's okay," Christine reassured Jamie and Casey. Of course, they didn't seem overly concerned. They'd probably assumed she was perfectly fine all along, just getting a shot or a checkup or some everyday sort of thing. But Christine was so happy that she hugged them both. "It looks like we'll be having a Merry Christmas after all."

124

13

"I can't believe this would happen only two days before the Christmas party." Felicity frowned as she pulled out yet another imitation evergreen garland from her apparently bottomless bag and handed it to Christine. Then she turned back to where she was arranging about a dozen red candles along with porcelain elves and reindeer on the fireplace mantle.

"Oh, Felicity," Aunt Hattie said from her position on the couch, where she was untangling a string of white lights. "These things happen. Let's just be thankful it wasn't more serious."

Christine returned to her current assignment without saying a word. She, for one, was getting a little weary of Felicity's complaints. Would she have been happier if Grandmother had been seriously ill? It seemed Felicity's biggest concern right now was not having anything ruin *her* party.

Christine may have been out of sight, but she was still

within hearing distance. Even so, she tried to block out Felicity's words as she attempted to wind another length of that stubborn garland around the staircase banister. It was like wrestling with a long, green monster.

"Well, I don't see why she had to go traipsing off to the cemetery clear over in Larchwood just days before Christmas."

"She just learned that her daughter is dead," Aunt Hattie said in a weary voice.

"I know, I know. And I'm sorry, really, I am, Aunt Hattie. But then Jimmy said that everyone has suspected as much for years. I think she just needs to let the past go and move on with her life. She has plenty of relatives around here who are alive and well. In fact, she's even got more than she knew she had." Felicity lowered her voice now, but this probably served only to attract more of Christine's attention. "What do you think she came here for, anyway?"

"To meet her family, I suspect."

"But why now?"

"Why not?"

"Well, did you know that she pretended to be someone else when she first came here? She acted like she was taking a job as Mom's caregiver."

Aunt Hattie just laughed. She had a sweet, merry laugh too. It reminded Christine of jingle bells, and probably helped her to suppress the urge to go out there and set Felicity straight. As a result of her frustration, she was probably wrapping the garland too tightly. Felicity had warned her not to do that. "Just gently drape it," she'd instructed. "But make the drapes hang evenly."

Although Christine had known Felicity for only a couple of weeks, she realized that she wasn't mean spirited as much as she was simply thoughtless. But thoughtless people had always aggravated Christine. Besides that, she didn't see why Felicity was so consumed with this party. Wasn't it enough that loved ones were going to gather together? Did every single detail have to be perfect too? Christine really wished Felicity would just lighten up and relax a little.

"You just need to take Felicity with a grain of salt sometimes," Grandmother had quietly told Christine as she had helped get the tired woman ready for bed earlier that evening. Of course, this was only after Felicity had implied that today's emergency trip to the hospital might've been partially Christine's fault.

"We all say things we don't mean sometimes," Grandmother had said sadly. "Goodness knows I've done it enough times." She'd leaned back into the pillows and closed her eyes. "I probably know better than anyone how words are hard to retract."

Christine hadn't known how to respond to that. She knew that Grandmother was still grieving over Lenore, and despite her assurance to everyone that all was well, she still seemed troubled. Deeply troubled. Christine hoped that a good night's rest might help her to get past whatever it was that seemed to be haunting her. Hopefully, she would be able to enjoy the festivities Felicity seemed bound and determined were going to happen.

"I invited twenty people," Felicity had told Christine when she came back out from attending to her grandmother. "And I need all the help I can get to pull this thing off. You promised me you'd help, Christine. I hope you're not backing out now."

And so Christine had stayed late stringing garlands and hanging lights and decorating a tall spruce tree that dominated the entire living room. Felicity had even gone so far as to remove the recliner and stick it in a dark, out of the way corner. Christine wondered what Grandmother would say about all this in the morning. Fortunately, the staircase was Christine's last assignment. Felicity had told her she was free to leave when it was done. *Free to leave!* As if she was the hired help. But then isn't that what she'd been masquerading as? Perhaps she was only getting her just dues now.

Christine had immediately liked Aunt Hattie. Of course, that was only her first impression of the little old woman, but Christine had found that her first impressions were often fairly accurate. Aunt Hattie was short and rotund with an equally round face. She had red tinted hair and sparkling blue eyes along with a quick smile that seemed genuine. She had appeared happy to meet Christine, hugged her warmly, and welcomed her to the family. Naturally, Hattie, like Jimmy and his family, was no actual relation to Christine, but she made her feel loved and accepted just the same.

"I was so sorry to hear about your ordeal with poor Esther today," she had told Christine. "Good land, it must've been terribly stressful for you. I'm so glad she's okay."

But their conversation had been cut short by Felicity's list of chores. Christine thought that Felicity, despite her sweet, blond appearance, would've made a good army sergeant.

At last Christine's portion of the list was completely done, and with only a quick "See you tomorrow," she was out the door and on her way back to the dorm.

But she wasn't prepared for the loveliness that greeted her outside. It had been just starting to snow when she'd driven her grandmother home from the hospital that afternoon, but it had stuck and by now accumulated what looked like almost two inches. Enough to transform their normally attractive college town into a beautiful winter wonderland. Streetlights reflected off the snow and made the night seem much brighter and more cheerful than usual. Christine felt like a little kid as she practically danced through the streets toward the dorm. And she knew just what she was going to do when she got to her room. She had a plan to make her grandmother a special Christmas gift.

It took her a while to locate the right box in her closet. She'd used most of this space to store boxes and items she hadn't wanted to put into storage with her father's things. But she finally found the precious box of old family photos her father had asked her to keep safe while he was out of the country. And she didn't think he'd mind if she shared some of these snapshots with her grandmother since they still had all the negatives for them.

By midnight she'd made a nice little stack of pictures of herself as a baby, a toddler, a young girl, and so on. She made sure that some of these shots included her parents, because it seemed important that her grandmother see and appreciate their role in her life. She wanted to reassure her grandmother that, despite Lenore giving her up for adoption, she'd still had a wonderful life and been loved by a pair of sweet, if slightly old-fashioned, parents. She hoped this would somehow help her grandmother resolve the inner conflict that seemed to be eating at her regarding Lenore. Oh, she knew it wouldn't fix everything. Only God could do something as big as that. But it might help a bit.

Tomorrow she'd go to the campus bookstore and get the perfect little album to contain these photos, and then she'd have something really special to present to Grandmother for Christmas. Of course, she'd still need to find something for Jimmy and his family, and Aunt Hattie too. But that might prove fun. She'd never had many relatives to buy presents for in the past. And she'd already sent her father his gift weeks ago to ensure its arrival. She'd carefully packed a box with some of the local foods, like raspberry jam and Starbucks coffee, things he had mentioned missing. And on top she'd tucked in a video Brianna had made of her before Christmas break. There were shots of her in their messy dorm room and around and about on campus. Christine knew her father would probably love the video even more than the food.

Finally Christine went to bed. She knew that tomorrow would be a demanding day. Felicity would probably have more lists, twice as long as tonight's, for her. But even so, she had a hard time going to sleep. She prayed for her father and then her grandmother and then everyone else she could think of, and finally, after what seemed hours, she drifted to sleep.

14

At last Esther's house was quiet. Felicity must've finally given up on her infernal decorating and gone home, and it sounded like Hattie had finally decided to call it a night too. Oh, why in the world had she ever agreed to let Hattie be her houseguest? It was bad enough that Felicity had insisted on having her ridiculous party here, but Esther was beginning to think that her family was trying to torture her. Just how much could an old woman take?

Knowing that sleep would be avoiding her, Esther pushed herself up into a sitting position on her bed and turned on her bedside light. Thankfully, Christine had left the crutches propped within reach. At least someone seemed to be looking out for her interests. That was something. She struggled to put on her robe, then slowly made her way out into the living room.

"Good heavens!" she exclaimed, then instantly regretted it, since Hattie was sleeping in the room down the hall. All these decorations for a little Christmas party!

What went on in Felicity's brain was a total mystery to Esther. Greenery and ribbons and baubles and bangles and every possible Christmas trinket were draped and hung from every pillar and post. She shook her head. Leave it to Felicity to try to take this thing right over the top. Of course, she'd assured her stressed-out daughter-in-law that everything was perfectly fine and that she should go right along with the party as planned, but she'd secretly hoped that Felicity would think better of it, especially considering the circumstances. Or at least tone down her plans a bit. But, no, Felicity was a headstrong young woman, and she seemed bound and determined to have the party of the year despite how her mother-in-law felt.

Esther went over to her desk. Even it was adorned with candles and greenery, and to her dismay the photograph of Lenore was nowhere to be seen. She checked in the bottom drawer, but it wasn't there either. Frustrated and feeling like a hostage in her own home, which had suddenly turned into Santa's Village, she flopped down in her desk chair, almost causing it to tumble. Well, it might just serve them right if she toppled right over and broke her neck. How would that make Felicity feel? Esther suspected that she'd probably go ahead and host the party without her.

Esther leaned back and tried to remember Lenore's face. Her big, brown eyes, so similar to Christine's, her sweet features. Oh, she'd been such a pretty girl. Perhaps that was what had gotten her into trouble in the first place. Naturally, the boys would be attracted to someone like her. Why hadn't Esther thought to warn her daughter? Why had she saved her motherly counsel until it was too late?

Esther still remembered that hot confrontation, almost as if it had happened today.

"How could you do this to me?" she'd demanded of her daughter all those years ago. It was only a week before high school graduation, and she'd just taken Lenore to the doctor and learned the news that her eighteen-year-old daughter was pregnant.

"To *you*?" Lenore had looked indignant as she slumped down in the passenger seat, arms folded tightly across her chest as if she wanted to shut out the entire world. "What about *me*, Mom? What about *my* life?"

"You should've considered that a few months ago," Esther had shot back at her. "I guess we should just be thankful that you're not showing yet. You can simply graduate as planned, and then we'll tell everyone you're going to tour Europe as a graduation gift." She'd laughed. "But we'll send you out to stay with Aunt Hattie instead. And that way you can just quietly get rid of it out there. No one will be the wiser. And, hopefully, you'll have learned your lesson by the time you get home."

"Get rid of it?" Lenore's expression had been horrified.

"Well, you know what I mean. You'll have an abortion, Lenore. Girls do it all the time. And it's perfectly legal where Aunt Hattie lives. I'm sure she might even know of a good doctor, since her late husband was a physician, you know. It's really quite simple."

"Quite simple?" Lenore had firmly shaken her head. "It might sound quite simple to you, Mother." Lenore called her *Mother* only when she was very angry. "But I refuse to kill another human being just to make my life more comfortable."

"It's not a human being," Esther had assured her daughter. "It's just fetal tissue. And it's easily disposed of."

"Disposed of?" Lenore's voice had gotten louder, and Esther had been thankful to be in the car. "Look, Mother," she'd told her, "I am not the least bit happy to know that I'm pregnant, but like it or not there's another human life involved now. And I am *not* going to just kill it to make everyone feel better." She'd started crying then, turning away from her mother and facing the passenger door. "I couldn't live with myself . . ."

Well, she should've known her daughter might pull something like this. After all, this was the girl who couldn't bear to kill a spider even when it was in the house. No, she would go find a cup, gently scoop it up, then transport it outside to its freedom. This was the girl who had rescued a fallen baby bird and climbed the tree to return it to its nest, nearly breaking her own neck in the process.

"I know this is hard for you, Lenore." Esther had decided to try a more gentle approach. "But maybe you should just trust me with the details for now. Perhaps I can go with you to Aunt Hattie's. We can make it a fun trip if you like. We'll do some shopping and—"

"No." Lenore's normally soft chin had become firm. "I am not going to kill my baby and then go out shopping as my reward. It's just not going to happen, Mom. I don't want to discuss it anymore."

Naturally, Esther hadn't given up. The very next day, she'd stopped by the Planned Parenthood office on campus. She'd discreetly worn dark glasses and had a scarf over her head as she picked up some brochures that explained the simple abortion procedure. She'd left these on the dresser in Lenore's room. Just a subtle hint. And it wouldn't hurt Lenore to read the facts about this simple procedure. She'd even called Hattie and, trusting her sister-in-law's discretion, told her the whole story. Of course, Hattie had been shocked and dismayed to learn of her niece's "promiscuous" behavior, as she had put it, but she'd also promised to keep Lenore at her home as long as needed.

The week before graduation had passed slowly, and Esther had felt that she and Lenore were playing some sort of game as they prepared for and attended various graduation events, both of them pretending that nothing whatsoever was wrong. Naturally, James had been absolutely no help. But then Lenore wasn't his daughter, and Esther had assumed that he was blaming her for her daughter's downfall. As a result, he'd barely spoken to either of them after he'd learned the embarrassing news. And then he'd taken off unexpectedly with the baseball coach to scout some young man with a "fastball in Peoria." He hadn't even attended Lenore's graduation. But that hadn't been such a surprise, considering his stepdaughter's wayward behavior. Esther hadn't held it against him.

It was a couple of days after graduation that the fireworks came out again. Esther had worked it out to take Lenore to Hattie's. They would fly out together the following week on the pretense of a little European vacation. She'd already been telling her friends that this was a plan to surprise her daughter. By the time the two of them returned later in the summer, no one in town would be the wiser. Even James had agreed that it was a good solution to an embarrassing situation. After all, he did have his image to protect.

But when she'd come home from the travel agent's office, airline tickets in hand, she'd discovered Lenore and James engaged in a horrible argument.

"You're a monster!" Lenore had screamed at her stepfather. "You should be thrown into prison and—"

"Listen to reason," he'd said in a loud voice. "You're acting completely foolish, Lenore. Your mother is only trying to help—"

"Help me murder a poor unborn baby?" she'd yelled back. "Clean up this unfortunate mess so the important Dr. Daniels can get back to his life without anyone knowing—"

"Lenore!" Esther had stormed in and scolded her daughter. "How dare you speak to your stepfather in that voice? Apologize to him at once."

But Lenore had turned and glared at her mother. It was an expression Esther had never seen on her daughter's face before, and one that would be forever etched in her memory.

"Apologize to him?" Lenore had shrieked. "That horrible monster should be apologizing to me."

"Lenore!" Esther had been completely shocked.

"That's right, Mother!" Lenore had held up her hands. "Go ahead. Take his side. I knew you would." Then she'd stormed off to her room and slammed the door.

Esther had apologized profusely to James, trying to explain how hormones could set a pregnant woman off, assuring him that everything would be okay once she got Lenore off to Hattie's.

But Lenore was gone the next morning. Naturally, Esther had assumed that she'd be back in time to fly out to Hattie's. After she'd had time to cool off a bit and think things through. She'd return to her mother, sorry and contrite and ready to go take care of this unfortunate business. But the following week passed, and then summer passed, and Lenore never came home.

"She's eighteen going on nineteen," James had reassured Esther when she'd suggested they declare her a missing person. "She doesn't have to come home if she doesn't want to. Maybe it's better like this, Esther. Maybe she needs to deal with this in her own way. You know she'll come back in time, when she's ready."

And Esther had listened to him and believed him. But one year followed the next, and Lenore never came home. At one point Esther had even considered hiring a private detective to search for her daughter, but by then pride and bitterness had begun to set in, and she'd decided to see who had more staying power—her or her daughter?

She sighed and leaned back in her desk chair. Now it was too late. Lenore was never coming home again. Death had separated them forever.

"Would you have returned, Lenore?" Esther asked the question aloud. "Would you have come back home to me if you had lived?"

She felt hot tears running down her cheeks again. How many tears had she cried in the past twenty-four hours? She felt like an old sponge that had been squeezed and wrung dry. How could she possibly have any tears left? Her heart ached as if someone had plucked it from her chest and torn it into pieces. How could a mother endure such pain? It was wrong, wrong, wrong to lose a child like this. But it was even more wrong to lose a child who had been estranged.

"I'm so sorry, Lenore," Esther whispered. "I was wrong and stupid. Please forgive me. I'm sorry . . ."

Her nose was dripping now, and she started jerking open her desk drawers in search of a tissue or handkerchief. But she stopped when she saw the small black book Jimmy had given her when his father died. It was lying on top of some papers in a drawer. Oh, she knew it was a Bible. But what on earth he'd thought she'd ever want with something like that was beyond her. She had no use for such religious relics. In fact, she thought she'd thrown the silly thing away long ago. For some reason, she picked it up now. She ran her finger over the gold embossed lettering of her name. Esther Louise Daniels. She supposed it was a sweet gesture on Jimmy's part. But then he'd always been a good boy. Maybe he wasn't her own flesh and blood, but he'd always treated her with such love and loyalty.

She opened the book, fanning through the delicate pages. Suddenly she remembered the last words on Lenore's gravestone. *John 3:16.* She had suspected at the time that they might be indicative of something from the Bible, but being generally unfamiliar with Bibles, the name and numbers meant nothing to her. Yet, for some unexplainable reason, they had remained in her mind. Perhaps this was meant to be a message for her, a message from beyond the grave, from her beloved daughter.

It took Esther a while before she figured things out and actually discovered where she might find this mysterious message. But finally she put her finger on what had to be it. She read the verse silently at first, and then aloud, pondering over each word.

"For God so loved the world that He gave His only begotten Son, that whoever believes in Him should not perish but have everlasting life."

She pulled out the satin ribbon that was sewn into the Bible and slipped it between the pages to mark the verse. Then she closed the book and leaned back in her chair and wondered. Was it really possible to have everlasting life? Could a person actually live forever? And who would want to? Good grief, she was so tired sometimes, like tonight for instance, that she wished she would simply go to sleep and never wake up again. Not ever.

But what if? What if there really was such a thing as everlasting life? A heaven, even? What if her beautiful Lenore was up there right now, perhaps even looking down and watching her? What if there was a way to see her daughter again, to tell her she was so very, very sorry, to tell her that she loved her, had always loved her? Oh, it was almost too much to imagine, too much to hope for. Too good to be true.

Esther pushed herself to her feet, left the Bible on her desk, and slowly made her way back to her bed. But before she went to sleep, she made a feeble attempt at prayer. Just in case God was really there and actually listening.

"I'm a foolish old woman," she said. "I don't even know how to say a proper prayer. But if what I just read in that black book is true, and if there really is some sort of life that goes on after death, then would you please show me what I must do to have it?" She wondered if she should add anything else, then finally said, "Amen."

Of course, she felt skeptical and slightly childish. But, she reminded herself, it might be better to ask the question and be wrong than to never ask at all.

15

Christine slept later than usual the next morning. Feeling guilty, she jerked on her clothes and then jogged through the snow, hurrying to her grandmother's house. It was close to nine, and she hoped she hadn't been missed yet. Although it seemed unlikely.

She knew Felicity was especially counting on her help today. Not only with the party preparations but also with Aunt Hattie's visit. Christine wondered if her grandmother's activities yesterday might have made her more tired than usual. Perhaps she'd decided to sleep in today. Otherwise, she'd probably be upset that Christine was late.

Christine let herself into the house and hurried into the living room.

"About time you got here," Felicity said as she set a cup of coffee next to her mother-in-law. "I already took care of Mom for you."

"I'm sorry," Christine said as she took off her coat.

"I didn't sleep very well last night and I woke up late and—"

"Oh, don't worry about it," her grandmother said. "Felicity is just getting herself too worked up over this confounded Christmas party. She thinks everything has to be picture perfect."

"Not perfect," Felicity said as she jotted something down on her ever-growing list. "Just nice."

"Have you had your breakfast yet, Grandmother?" Christine asked.

"No, she hasn't," Felicity said quickly. "And neither has Aunt Hattie. You take care of that, Christine, and I'll make a quick run to the store. Then I want you to start on that list that I've left for you in the kitchen. Okay?"

Christine nodded and went into the kitchen to discover that Felicity had initiated some sort of major baking project that had left bowls, measuring utensils, and various ingredients strewn across every countertop. Christine located her list in the midst of this mess and, blowing off the flour, read the first chore: "Clean the kitchen."

Christine shook her head as she cleared enough space on the counter to begin fixing breakfast. First things first. She found ham in the refrigerator and cut some slices, then poached enough eggs for the two older women as well as herself. If Felicity planned to work her like a dog today, she would at least fortify herself with a good breakfast.

She decided to serve breakfast in the dining room for a change, and searched until she found three placemats that matched the blue willow dishes she'd admired in the cabinet. When the food was done and the table was set, she went out to announce, "Breakfast is served in the dining room," as if she were an English butler.

Her grandmother chuckled. "Does that mean I have to get out of my chair?"

"Do you mind?" Christine asked tentatively. "I thought since we had a guest . . ."

"I think it would be lovely to eat in the dining room," her grandmother said. Christine blinked in surprise but said nothing.

Aunt Hattie came into the room. "We're eating in the dining room?" she asked in a cheerful voice.

"Yes," Esther said. "My granddaughter thinks we should dine in style this morning."

And so they did. Christine had already opened the drapes to reveal the beautiful white blanket that had turned the backyard into a sparkling winter wonderland.

"This is lovely," Aunt Hattie said. "What a nice treat."

"Christine is a good cook too," Esther said as she leaned her crutches against the table and maneuvered herself into the chair at the head of the table. "She used to cook and clean for her father after her mother passed away."

"And your father?" Aunt Hattie asked. "Is he still alive?"

Christine explained about Brazil, and Aunt Hattie smiled. "Oh, that must be wonderful. I've often wished I could go do something like that."

"Why don't you?" Christine asked.

"Don't you think I'd be too old?"

"My father is sixty-four," Christine said. "You can't be much older than that."

Aunt Hattie laughed. "Well, now, aren't you a sweet

thing." She winked at Esther. "If you ever get tired of her, just feel free to send her my way."

"Humph." Esther grunted as she reached for a second piece of toast. "You don't need to worry yourself about that, Hattie. Christine and I get along just fine, thank you very much."

Christine tried to keep the chatter light after that. She didn't like the idea of the two women getting riled up about some old offense during the breakfast she had so carefully prepared. Fortunately, they didn't. Perhaps Jimmy had been right after all. Maybe Aunt Hattie had simply come to help bury the hatchet.

She left the two women to their coffee and returned to her task of cleaning the kitchen. She was just finishing up when Felicity came blasting through the back door with a full load of groceries. "There's more in the car," she told Christine.

Christine restrained herself from saluting her drill sergeant aunt. Instead she turned to dry her hands, then went out to the garage to retrieve several more bags of groceries from the open trunk. How many people was Felicity expecting anyway?

"But why do you need to call your lawyer *today*, Mom?" Felicity was asking when Christine came back inside.

Christine set the bags on the counter and paused to listen. Not that she really wanted to eavesdrop, but Felicity's voice sounded more aggravated than usual.

"I have my reasons," Esther said in a sharp voice. "I only asked you to bring me the phone and my phonebook, Felicity. I didn't expect you to put me through the Spanish Inquisition."

"I just wondered," Felicity said. "Hang on, Mom, I'll go get the cordless for you."

Christine continued unloading the groceries from the bags, taking time to sort things a bit and putting the cold things in the refrigerator.

"Is that it?" Felicity asked when she came back into the kitchen.

Christine nodded. "That was everything in your trunk."

"Did you get that box from the backseat too?"

Christine wondered if Felicity thought she was her personal slave. "No, I didn't know there was any—"

"It's the napkins and plates and things," Felicity said. She glanced over her shoulder to the dining room. "Can you get them right now, please?"

So Christine returned to the garage to retrieve the box. She suspected that Felicity wanted to get rid of her for a minute or two, and when she returned she noticed Felicity standing motionless next to the swinging doors that led to the living room, where Grandmother was talking on the phone, presumably to her attorney. It seemed that Felicity was listening. So Christine dropped the cardboard box on the counter with a loud thud that made Felicity jump.

Christine smiled at her aunt. "Anything else?"

Felicity seemed momentarily stumped, but she quickly recovered. "Yes. We need the walks shoveled. There's nearly three inches of snow out there."

This time Christine actually did salute. "Aye-aye, ma'am," she said in what she hoped would be taken as good humor.

Then she headed to the closet for her parka and to search out a snow shovel. She actually felt relieved to escape the house and Felicity's never-ending list of demands. Outside the air was fresh and brisk, and Christine felt that nothing was more invigorating than shoveling snow on a crisp, sunny day. She took her time to carefully clear all the walks and the sidewalk and driveway before she finally went back into the house. She was just hanging her parka back in the hall closet when she heard voices coming from the guest room where Aunt Hattie was staying.

"I just don't get it, Aunt Hattie," said Felicity in an urgent tone.

"What's that, dear?" Aunt Hattie asked in her usual cheerful voice.

"Why Mom suddenly wants to change her will."

"Most likely it's because she knows she has a grand-daughter now."

"But why just two days before Christmas?"

"I don't really know, dear. Perhaps she's worried about her health."

"But we don't even know that Christine is really related. I mean, she hasn't done a blood test or anything."

"Oh, Felicity." Aunt Hattie's voice was an odd mix of frustration layered with patience. "We can all see that Christine is Lenore's daughter. I realize that you never knew Lenore, dear, but believe me, we can all see it plain as day. It's right there in Christine's eyes . . . and in her spirit. Oh, the two of them may not look that much alike, but she is definitely Lenore's flesh and blood. I have absolutely no doubt of that."

"Even so," Felicity persisted, "it just doesn't seem fair."

"What's that, dear?"

"That Mom should suddenly change the will. I mean, everything she has, this house and, well, whatever . . .

didn't it all come from Jimmy's dad in the first place? The way I understood it was that the Daniels side had all the money."

"All the money . . ." Aunt Hattie sighed.

Christine suddenly felt guilty for listening in. Why, she'd just gotten irritated after catching Felicity doing the same thing with Grandmother's phone conversation. And here she was doing it herself. Just the same, she couldn't seem to make herself leave.

"I know, I know," Felicity continued. "And I know I probably sound petty and greedy to you. But does it seem fair to you that a perfect stranger should walk in and claim to be a relative and then Mom goes off changing her will?"

"Oh, Felicity," Aunt Hattie said.

Suddenly Christine couldn't take it anymore. Not only did she know that it was wrong to eavesdrop, but she realized it was painful too. She turned and walked toward the living room.

"There you are," Esther said as she hobbled toward her.

"Grandmother," Christine said in surprise, hoping that her face didn't look too guilty.

"You look flushed, Christine. Are you all right?"

She forced a smile. "I've been outside shoveling snow."

"Good for you." Her grandmother struggled to balance on her crutches as she fished around in her sweater pocket for something. Then she held out a closed fist as if she had a surprise in her hand. "Something for you."

Christine held out her open hand and waited as her grandmother dropped a small brass key. "What's this?"

146

Her grandmother glanced up the staircase. "It's the key to Lenore's room. Second door on the left."

Christine nodded.

"I never changed a single thing after she left. I guess I always thought she'd come back someday, and I wanted it to look just the same as before she left. As if I'd been expecting her to come home. I even had a deadbolt lock installed years ago. Just to make sure no one could go in and disturb anything." She shook her head sadly. "I'd go up there with you now if I could just handle those stairs—"

"Oh, no, you don't need to do that."

"Yes. It's probably better that I don't." She sighed. "Anyway, I thought you might want to see her room and her things, you know, perhaps get a better idea of who she was. I suppose we should eventually clear those old things out. It's not as if I want it to become some sort of shrine or anything. I just wanted it to be there for her . . ."

Christine sensed her grandmother's pain. "Maybe I could help box her things up for you, Grandmother."

"Yes, that would be good."

"Maybe I could do it after Christmas. I know our church is always looking for clothing items for our homeless shelter."

"Good." Her grandmother nodded. "I figured you might have some ideas. And then, Christine, once it's all cleared out . . . Well, I thought maybe you'd like to use it for yourself. I mean, it's really a lovely room, with its own bath and a balcony that overlooks the backyard and pool." She smiled in a sad way. "Of course, I don't expect you to live here. Goodness only knows why anyone would want to stay with a decrepit old woman like me. But I want you to know that you're welcome to use that room anytime you like."

"Thank you." Christine was trying to think of adequate words to describe how she would be perfectly happy, thrilled even, to live in this lovely house with her grandmother, but before she could speak her grandmother turned away.

"Now I've got some business to attend to." She started moving down the hall again. "I'll be in James's study if anyone needs me."

Christine wondered why her grandmother still called that room "James's study." Perhaps it was simply out of respect for her deceased husband. Christine had peeked in to admire the dark-paneled room with its floor-to-ceiling bookcases one day. She'd always thought it would be so lovely to have a library like that. Yet the room had such a rigid formality to it, so much so that she hadn't felt quite welcome in there. She'd also noticed that her grandmother seldom used the room and kept her own desk in a corner of the living room. Perhaps she didn't feel quite welcome in there either.

16

Christine began to climb the stairs, careful not to disturb the evergreen garland she'd so painstakingly draped there the other day. She'd been upstairs a few times before. Just to vacuum and dust, and once to look for an old book her grandmother had thought was in one of the bedrooms up there. She'd noticed that closed door with the deadbolt lock and wondered. But she hadn't asked. Even so, she'd figured it had something to do with Lenore.

She slipped the key into the lock and turned it. Feeling like an intruder, she went inside. She stood by the door, looking around and simply taking it all in. It's not that she believed in ghosts or anything like that, but it was as if she could feel a presence or an aura or something almost tangible. She actually held her breath for a moment as she listened to the silence and tried to imagine an eighteen-year-old Lenore moving through this pretty room.

The spacious room had daintily flowered wallpaper in pastel shades of peach and green that ran up the walls above the wainscoting. Old-fashioned framed prints of fairies playing among flowers and pretty girls in gardens adorned the walls. Very feminine and very sweet. The furnishings all matched and were painted a creamy white that had been made to look old. The bed was covered in a patchwork quilt that reminded Christine of a spring garden just beginning to bloom.

She slowly walked over to the large bureau with a mirror on top. This was the only part of the room that seemed to show any clutter or actual use. Here she found all sorts of high school memorabilia—all covered in a thick layer of dust. A pair of red and gold pom-poms, a yearbook, several awards, graduation announcements, photos of friends, a gold graduation tassel . . . all the bits and pieces of an eighteen-year-old life. But suddenly Christine's eyes stopped when she came across a brochure. For some reason it seemed completely out of place. The words *unwanted pregnancy* seemed to glare at her in bold black and white. Christine picked up the brochure, shook off about two decades worth of accumulated dust, and read a few lines. It seemed to be a clinical explanation of how an abortion was a "safe and efficient way to terminate an unwanted pregnancy." Christine set the brochure back down, placing it exactly where it had been before, the outline clearly visible in the layers of dust. She knew she was the reason the brochure was on the bureau.

So her birth mother had actually considered an abortion. Christine's hand went up to her throat and her chest tightened as the word *unwanted* seemed to echo through her entire being. Suddenly she realized that she had been and still was a great inconvenience to this family. She considered Felicity's words just moments ago; her attitude toward Christine had seemed to reflect this same attitude. And now as Christine stood there—in her dead birth mother's room, in her grandmother's house, among people who were virtually strangers to her—it seemed quite obvious. Everything about this was all wrong. Why had she even come here in the first place? What was her motive? And why had she forced her way into a world where she clearly did not fit in? A world where she hadn't even been wanted. Not then. Not now.

She started for the door, ready to run, escape from this place. But then she paused. She took a deep breath and attempted to calm and steady herself. Perhaps she was overreacting. And, certainly, she'd been through a lot during the past few weeks. Why not give herself some time to sort this all out? And even if Lenore had been considering an abortion, there obviously had been something that influenced her to change her mind. Christine was here, after all. That proved something.

Christine knew that *something* had caused Lenore to run away from her family home and then to carry her "unwanted" baby to full term. But perhaps that was also what had caused her death in the end. Perhaps if she'd stayed home with her family and gotten the abortion described in that brochure, perhaps Lenore would still be alive today. Not that Christine believed that abortions were right. She pressed her fingers against her forehead and tried to think. But it seemed too much to consider, too hard to understand, too painful, too confusing . . .

"Christine?"

Christine whirled around to see Aunt Hattie standing in the doorway.

Aunt Hattie smiled. "May I come in?"

Christine swallowed and nodded. "Of course."

Aunt Hattie looked around. "It looks just the same in here. Such a pretty room. Lenore picked out everything in here herself, you know. It was while James and Esther were honeymooning in the Bahamas. I stayed here at the house with Lenore while the newlyweds were gone. Lenore was only fifteen at the time, but James had given her permission to decorate the room however she liked. 'Spare no expense,' he'd told her right before the two of them took off." Aunt Hattie sighed happily.

Christine nodded, trying to catch some of the old woman's enthusiasm. "That must've been fun for her."

Aunt Hattie frowned. "I suppose. But it wasn't long before Lenore discovered that money isn't everything."

Christine nodded but said nothing.

"Mind if I sit down?" Aunt Hattie nodded to a white wooden rocking chair next to the bed.

"Sure. But you might want to dust it off first."

But before she sat down Aunt Hattie closed the bedroom door. Then she went over and sat down on the chair without bothering about the dust. Her expression had become troubled, but she didn't say anything. Instead she sat there for what seemed like several minutes, just looking at Christine as if she was studying her. Or perhaps trying to figure her out. Christine felt uncomfortable and wondered again why she had tried to force her way into this family. Why didn't she just leave?

Finally Christine couldn't take any more silence. "Is

something wrong?" she asked. She sat down on the edge of the bed, directly across from Aunt Hattie, and waited.

"Well, that depends on how you look at it," she said.

Christine suspected this had to do with Felicity. Perhaps she had asked Aunt Hattie to speak to Christine today. Maybe they were going to ask her to get a blood test. Or demand to know why she was here. Or perhaps they wanted to ask her to leave. Christine simply waited.

"I have something to tell you that I feel you have the right to know." She sighed. "But this isn't easy for me."

Christine looked down at her hands folded neatly in her lap, Sunday school hands, her mother used to say, and she continued to wait. Whatever it was, she wished Aunt Hattie would just spit it out. Get it over with.

"As you know, dear, Esther's second husband, James, was my little brother. He was only four years younger than me, but I always babied him as if I were much older. You see, our parents were very busy people. They were quite wealthy, and, as a result, they were always caught up in every social cause and function, and, well, we children were left to our own a lot. I suppose I became something of a mother hen to James. We were very close."

Christine looked curiously at Aunt Hattie. What did any of this have to do with her? But still she didn't say anything. Just waited for the old woman to continue.

"I'm sure you're wondering where I'm going with my little story." Aunt Hattie attempted a meek smile. "Well, as you can imagine, Esther, your grandmother, was very upset when Lenore became pregnant. Her plan was to send her to me for a while so that Lenore could have an abortion and then get on with her life."

Christine nodded. "I saw the brochure on Lenore's dresser."

She swallowed. "It's kind of hard to think about your birth mother wanting to—well, you know—abort you."

"Oh, no, no, no. Lenore didn't want an abortion at all. That was all Esther's idea. She felt it was a neat way to clean this whole mess up. Personally, I didn't much care for the idea myself, but then I knew enough to keep quiet."

"*Grandmother* wanted Lenore to have an abortion?"

"That's right. She was worried about James's reputation at the college. He was being considered for presidency at this time. And she didn't want anything to hurt his chances."

"Oh." Christine knew this made sense, but it still cut deeply to think that her own grandmother had wanted her life "terminated," as the brochure put it.

"Anyway, all this became moot when Lenore disappeared."

Christine nodded.

"But then something happened . . . ," she continued slowly, as if she wasn't sure how to say whatever it was she wanted to say, "shortly before my brother James died several years ago. Perhaps you've heard by now that he'd been diagnosed with an unusual form of cancer and given less than six months to live . . . Well, it was during that time that he wrote me several letters. At first I thought my little brother was losing his mind due to his terminal illness and the heavy pain medications, because the letters made absolutely no sense whatsoever to me. They were filled with remorse and regret and guilt. And yet, in my opinion, this was a man who had led an exemplary life. It made no sense."

Christine felt like she was getting an informational, not to mention emotional, overload today, and she just wished Aunt Hattie would get to the point. If there was a point. And right now she wasn't too sure.

Aunt Hattie reached in her pocket to remove a pink linen handkerchief with lace trim. "Then the final letter came . . . and in this particular letter James confessed that he'd been the one responsible for Lenore's pregnancy, which resulted in her subsequent disappearance. And he felt certain that his illness was his punishment for this transgression, and he wanted to tell Esther the truth, but he simply couldn't do it. Oh, believe me, it was a very, very sad letter indeed."

Christine just stared at her, too stunned to speak or respond. In fact, she felt her lips growing numb and wondered if she might actually be having some sort of stroke or seizure, although she knew that was probably ridiculous and highly unlikely. But how could she possibly have heard what she thought she'd just heard? Or maybe she'd simply misunderstood. "Wh—what?" she managed to stutter.

"I know it's shocking, dear, but I felt you had the right to know."

"What are you saying?" Christine winced at the words that were about to come from her mouth. "Are you saying that Lenore's stepfather is my birth father?"

Aunt Hattie nodded sadly, then dabbed her moist eyes with the corner of her handkerchief. "I'm sorry, dear, but that's what my brother wrote in his letter."

Christine's stomach twisted and turned, and she felt as if she was going to be sick. How could this be? It was so wrong. So unfair. Not only had this poor girl been judged and misunderstood by her own mother, but she'd been sexually abused by her stepfather as well. It was too painful and hideous to even think about. Christine longed to purge this tale from her mind and to run from this horrible house where such dirty little secrets had been hidden for so many years. What was wrong with these people?

"Oh, I know it's disturbing to hear this, dear. But I think it's best to just get these things out in the open and then move on. James fully admitted his guilt in his last letter to me. Yes, he admitted that he had raped his stepdaughter. And, of course, it was wrong. But you must keep this in perspective, dear. He'd been under enormous stress at work, and Esther had taken off to visit her sick mother and had been gone for weeks."

Christine listened to Aunt Hattie going on and on about how it had been spring break and how "poor James" had been doing some very heavy drinking and missing his wife. As if that excused such inexcusable behavior!

"Apparently the weather had been nice that week," Aunt Hattie rambled as if she was telling a bedtime story, "and Lenore had been swimming in the pool with her friends, and walking around the house in a very provocative bikini. Oh, I know that's no excuse, dear." She pressed her lips together, and Christine controlled herself from saying something very regrettable. *Just get this over with,* she was thinking. *Tell your story and be done with it!*

Finally Aunt Hattie continued. "There's really no easy way to understand these things, dear, but James admitted he was so intoxicated that he barely remembered what had happened that day. He wrote that Lenore had confronted him with it later, when she'd discovered she was pregnant, and that they'd gotten into quite an argument. Naturally, James tried to make himself believe that her accusations weren't true. Maybe he'd even managed to convince himself that it wasn't true over time. But I think that beneath it all, he always knew he'd done it. He knew he'd raped Lenore."

"That's so disgusting." Christine grimaced and tightened her fists. "That's like . . . like *incest*."

Aunt Hattie firmly shook her head. "No, dear, it's not actually incest since they weren't blood relatives."

"Well, my father isn't a blood relative either," Christine said hotly. "But if he ever did that to me—" She shuddered at what she knew was an impossibility. "Ugh, that would be just the same as incest to me."

"I know, I know. It's a horrible thing to hear. And if it makes you feel any better, James was completely heartbroken with regret over it. You can read his letters if you like. He would've done anything to turn back the clock and erase that awful day. And I have a feeling that it really did contribute to his illness and his death in the end."

"And Lenore's death too." Christine shook her head. "What a stupid, stupid waste."

"Not completely," Aunt Hattie said with a hopeful smile. "At least there's you."

Christine felt a large lump filling her throat now, making it hard to breathe, let alone respond. It was one thing to be an illegitimate child, an unwanted pregnancy, an embarrassing inconvenience. Although, in fact, she was still grappling with those unkind labels. But it was something entirely different to be the product of a violent crime, the result of rape that was practically incestuous. How would she ever reconcile herself to something like this? Suddenly she wanted her father more than ever. She wanted to pour out her troubles to him and have him comfort her and then just make everything go away.

"I've got to go." She quickly stood.

"Oh, I hope I didn't upset you, dear," Aunt Hattie said. "I only wanted you to know the truth. You seem like such a sensible girl to me. I thought you could handle it. Of course, I plan to tell Esther too, but I wanted to tell you first. I felt you had a right to know. You see, I tried to tell Esther once before and, well, it caused quite a scene."

"At the funeral?"

"Yes. But I think it's important that she knows and accepts the truth now that you're here. And, actually, once you adjust yourself to everything, well, it's not so bad, really."

Aunt Hattie stood and held her arms open wide as if she were expecting a big hug. But Christine was still too stunned to respond. She simply backed away.

"I've got—got to go," she said for the second time as she made her way to the door. "I'm—I'm sorry."

She dashed down the stairs, carelessly tearing a strip of garland loose on her way. She opened the closet and grabbed her parka, then shot out the front door without even closing it behind her. She could hear Felicity calling after her, probably wanting her to stuff a turkey or bake a pie or hang some mistletoe, but Christine was finished with all that Christmas nonsense now. More than that, she wanted to be finished with this crazy family as well.

17

Esther sat and stared blankly at the old letters splayed across James's normally orderly desktop. They looked almost as if the wind had blown them in. Or Hurricane Hattie. She should've known better than to let that crazy old woman into her home. Good grief, hadn't Hattie always been the bearer of bad news?

Oh yes, the letters appeared to have been written in James's handwriting, perhaps not as neatly as his usual smooth and controlled hand, but that was most likely due to his illness or the medications, and, of course, there'd been stress. And there was no doubt they'd been written on his own personal stationery embossed with his own initials, JD. And, of course, he wouldn't have used the college letterhead that he normally reserved for official work correspondence. And, most likely, he'd sat right here, right in this big leather chair, when he'd composed them.

But was the content really true? Poor James had endured some heavy pain medications during the last few months of his life. Perhaps those drugs had affected his mind. Maybe he'd even been hallucinating. These were the excuses she'd given Hattie shortly before she'd closed the door and barricaded herself in James's den with the sternest instructions: "I do not wish to be disturbed."

Once the door was locked and she was alone, she'd sat there and read and reread each letter until she'd nearly memorized each and every painful word. And now, despite her own earlier misgivings and doubts, she realized that the letters relayed the truth. James had indeed raped her only daughter. Oh, it was difficult to form those words in her mind. It sounded so crude and base and immoral. Not at all like the man she'd been happily married to for fifteen years. Just the same, she knew it was true.

Perhaps she'd always known. At least deep down in some hidden corner of her mother's heart. After all, hadn't Lenore tried to tell her without actually saying the words? But mired in her own foolish pride and stubbornness, Esther had refused to listen to her own daughter.

She leaned back into the chair and closed her eyes. Oh, the stupid and senseless messes people make of their lives. One mess leads smack into another and then another and another. It made her weary just thinking of it. It was like the redundancy of the seaside, one wave tumbling into the next. She had always grown tired of the sound of the ocean after a few days. James had never understood this. Maybe it was just her, since most people seemed to love the sound of the ocean, but the endless pounding of wave after wave after wave had always worn on her nerves. Just the way this whole nasty business with James was wearing on her now. His guilt only added more layers to her own guilt, making her feel worse than ever. And just when she'd been hoping for some resolution too. Oh, when would the hurting ever cease?

She looked at the photograph of James that she kept on his desk. It was taken shortly after he'd been selected as the university president. Such a proud day that had been. In fact, it would've been perfect except for the fact that Lenore was missing. She studied his smile and wondered how he'd really felt that day. Was he pleased with himself for the way he'd managed to conceal such a hideous offense? Or was he smiling like that simply to hide the shame?

Oh, she'd always known that James Daniels was a rather self-indulgent man. But then he'd been raised that way. Rich from birth, and always given everything, life had been easy come, easy go for him. And he'd always been the golden boy—the man with the Midas touch. Everyone who knew him had respected him. Even Lenore.

Esther choked back a sob as she remembered the evening, almost a year after she and James had married, when Lenore had come downstairs to tell them goodnight. Wearing flannel pajamas and a freshly scrubbed face, she'd said, "I don't know how to say this . . ." Lenore had paused then as if this was something very important to her. "But I'm really glad that you guys are married. I know I wasn't so excited at first because I didn't really think anyone could replace my daddy. But I think James is the next best thing, and if it's okay, I'd like to start calling you Dad." Well, James had jumped up from his chair and hugged her, saying that of course she could call him Dad and that he'd be proud to have her for his own daughter.

161

It was a tender moment then, but it burned like hellfire now.

"That beast!" Esther said as she pounded her fist on his desk. "That abominable monster!" She stood up, shaking her fist in the air. "How could you, James Allen Daniels? How dare you?" She hobbled around the desk, ignoring the pain of her throbbing ankle as it knocked against the leg of the chair. With angry sobs, she reached for his shining brass football trophy, the one he'd won in college, and then she threw it to the floor. Like a madwoman, she clung to the bookshelves and struggled her way around his office, taking every single item he'd been proud of, every award and honor he'd ever received, and one by one, she smashed them to the floor. Finally she took his photo, held it high above her head, and brought it down with a loud crash that sent glass flying across the desk. "You demon!"

"What's going on?" Felicity demanded as she loudly knocked on the door. "Are you okay, Mom?"

"I'm fine!" Esther shouted. "Perfectly fine. Just leave me alone!"

Finally, exhausted and in pain from her ankle, Esther collapsed onto the leather couch by the window and just sobbed. *Why, why, why?*

When she awoke, the room had grown dark and it took her a moment to remember where she was, but she thought she heard someone knocking on the door again. "Who is it?" she asked in a voice that sounded like an ancient toad.

"It's me," said an apologetic voice. But before Esther could get up, a key turned in the lock, the door opened, and the light came on. And there stood Hattie looking around the room with an expression of horror. "My word, Esther, whatever has happened in here?"

Esther sat up and rubbed her eyes. "A little temper tantrum."

"Do you feel better now?" Hattie asked with what seemed genuine concern.

"As a matter of fact, I do." Esther looked at the mess, then just shook her head. "Can you hand me my crutches, Hattie?"

Hattie carefully picked her way through the broken glass and debris to retrieve the crutches, then leaned them against the couch beside Esther. "I don't blame you, Esther," she said as she sat down beside her. "You know that James was my only brother and that I loved him dearly, but, believe me, I wanted to kill him myself when I read that last letter."

Esther blinked, then looked at her sister-in-law. "Really?"

Hattie nodded. "Yes, if he hadn't been terminally ill, I might have."

Esther shook her head again.

"And if he hadn't been in such bad shape, I probably wouldn't have forgiven him either."

"But you did?"

She sighed. "I did. It's hard to deny mercy to a dying man. In the end I actually felt rather sorry for him. Oh, I couldn't excuse his behavior, there's no excuse for that. But I do think it's what killed him. I believe the guilt was eating him alive and the cancer was simply his body's way of surrendering to it."

"He said something like that in his letters."

"Poor man."

"Poor Lenore," Esther said.

Hattie patted Esther's hand. "Yes, poor, dear Lenore. She was such a sweet angel of a girl. She certainly didn't deserve that kind of treatment."

"No one does," Esther said sadly.

"Did I ever tell you that your girl won my heart right from the start?" Hattie said. "Why, I still remember the first day I met her, just a few days before the wedding, and she gave me the sweetest little tour of this house. Well, I took her into my heart as if she were my very own niece that very day. She was precious, Esther."

Esther started choking up again. "I—I know."

"And my, but she loved you. I remember how she was slightly brokenhearted after the two of you left for your honeymoon. Oh, but she missed her mommy."

"Did she?"

"My, yes. I did everything I could think of to cheer her up, including driving to every furniture store in the county until we found the bedroom set of her dreams to distract her."

"You were a good aunt to her, Hattie."

"Well, thank you."

"I feel so guilty," Esther said. "Lenore tried to tell me it was James, but I just wouldn't listen. I told myself she was simply trying to blame us for her making bad choices and getting into trouble. But, beneath it all, I think I suspected something was wrong. Still, it was too horrible to actually believe. I mean, how could he do—" She shook her head as the words choked inside her.

Hattie wrapped her short arms around Esther and squeezed tightly. "I know, I know," she said. "It just makes no sense at all. But life is like that sometimes, Esther. And like I told Christine earlier, we can at least be thankful that we have her now. I think she's our blessing in disguise in this whole unfortunate affair."

"Christine," Esther said suddenly. "She knows about this?"

Hattie nodded. "It seemed only fair to tell her. And since James had written the letter to me, and I am, after all, her blood relative, her aunt, I thought it best I tell her. I figured you'd be enduring a pain all your own today."

Esther nodded. "Yes, perhaps you're right about that. But how did she take the news? Was she shocked or upset?"

"Yes. I think it was unsettling for her. She left here in a hurry." Then Hattie smiled. "But don't worry, she's young. The young have a way of bouncing back from these sorts of things. She probably just needs some time to sort it out."

Esther frowned. "I'm not so sure. She's so much like Lenore. She has a very tender heart, and this might be very disturbing to her."

"Maybe you're right. Should you give her a call and see how she's doing?"

"Yes. That's what I'll do." Esther started to stand.

"Wait," Hattie said as she bent over to pick up the dented football trophy and set it on the side table. "Let me clear you a safe path first. In fact, why don't you go call from another room while I straighten this place up a bit?"

"Oh, you don't need to—"

"Nonsense, dear. I want to."

So Esther hobbled out to the living room and sat down at her desk to search for Christine's number. Finally she found it and dialed. She glanced at her watch as the phone rang several times. It was almost six o'clock and no one was answering. Perhaps Christine had gone out with friends tonight. Maybe to some holiday party. The girl was certainly entitled to her own activities. Esther considered leaving a message, then, unsure of what to say, she simply hung up. Maybe Hattie was right. Maybe the poor girl just needed some time and space to get over this thing. Give her time. Surely, she'd be back by tomorrow.

"Felicity?" Esther called, thinking her daughter-in-law must still be around, probably off in the kitchen fussing with some fruitcake or appetizers for her infernal Christmas party, which, more than ever, Esther wished they could cancel now. But, to her surprise, no one answered, and Esther decided that Felicity must've finally gone home to her husband and children. Well, that was for the best.

Esther had just gotten to her feet and was about to go and see if she could stir up something for her and Hattie to eat for supper when it hit her. If Christine was James's daughter, that meant that she was Jimmy's half sister. Suddenly she realized she had a responsibility to tell him this news. She sat back down and dialed his number, and, thankfully, he answered the phone. She didn't think she could bear to have one more conversation with Felicity today!

"Hello, Jimmy," she said in an uncertain voice. "I have some news for you, but now I'm wondering if I shouldn't tell you face to face."

"Is something wrong, Mom?" His voice sounded concerned. "Felicity said you were acting a bit odd today."

"Not exactly wrong," she told him. "But it is something important. Are you kids in the middle of dinner right now?"

"Actually, I already fed the kids, and Felicity and I were just thinking of sending out for Chinese."

"Well, how about if you order enough for Hattie and me, my treat, of course."

"Sounds great. I felt bad that we didn't get to take Aunt Hattie out for dinner yesterday."

"I'm sure she'll enjoy it tonight just as much."

"How about Christine? Should I bring some for her too?"

"No, she's not here."

"Okay. I'll call it in now, and it'll probably be about seven thirty by the time we pick it up and get there. Is that all right?"

"That'll be fine." Esther hung up the phone and took in a slow breath. She hoped it would be fine. More likely than not, it would turn into a total mess.

18

Hattie and Esther had just finished setting the dining room table, complete with china, silver, cloth napkins, and even candles, which was Hattie's idea, when Jimmy and Felicity arrived with several white bags of food.

"That smells yummy," Hattie said as the two younger people arranged the little white cartons in the center of the table.

"Where are the kids?" Esther asked as she sat down at the head of the table, her usual position.

"My sister took them to a musical at her church," Felicity said.

Esther nodded. That was convenient, since she wasn't quite sure how to make kids understand what she had to say tonight.

The four of them made casual chitchat throughout dinner, but Esther could tell that Felicity was smoldering with curiosity. Esther wondered what Jimmy had told her, if anything. Her guess was that Felicity would be assuming this had to do with the revisions to her will, since she knew her daughter-in-law had been hovering around her for much of the day, most likely trying to eavesdrop on her conversation with her attorney. But all that would have to come later, when Christine was here too.

Jimmy leaned back in his chair and patted what was beginning to look like a slight paunch on his belly. "Mmm, that was good. Thanks, Mom."

Felicity sat straighter in her chair now, a forced smile gracing her pretty pink lips. "Jimmy said you have something to tell us."

Esther glanced at Hattie, who nodded as if to encourage her to begin. "Well, it's something of a long story that I'd prefer to tell in a slightly shorter version."

"Go ahead and shoot," Jimmy said.

"This won't be easy to hear," she began, "and, believe me, it's not easy to tell." She had decided to start this off gently, since James was Jimmy's father. So she began by explaining how James had been under a lot of stress twenty years ago, about how he'd been drinking too much, and so on. But finally she could tell by their bewildered faces that she might as well just cut to the chase.

"What I'm trying to say is that James . . . uh, well, James . . ." She cleared her throat and took a deep breath. "James raped my daughter, Lenore."

"What?" Jimmy just about leaped from his chair. "What are you saying?" He turned and looked at Hattie with wide eyes. "Is this true, Aunt Hattie?"

She nodded sadly. "I'm sorry to say that it is. I've known about this for years. I tried to tell Esther at James's funeral, but she just—"

"That's what that was about?" Jimmy's eyes were bright, and his face was flushed with emotion.

Esther felt a wave of pity for her stepson. "I'm sorry, Jimmy. Believe me, we've all been hurt by this."

"Not nearly as much as poor Lenore," Hattie said.

"How do you know this is true?" Felicity demanded in an ice-cold voice. "I mean, how dare you go about making these kinds of serious accusations against a man who's not even here to defend himself?" She pointed at Hattie. "You, his own sister?" And then she pointed at Esther. "And his widow?" She shook her head. "How dare you?" She stood up and started to cry. "And right before Christmas too. I think you just want to ruin Christmas, and my—my party. I think you are both—both—evil!" She ran from the room sobbing.

"Do you want to go to her?" Esther asked Jimmy in a weary voice.

He just shook his head and slowly exhaled. "She'll get over it."

"Now, I feel absolutely terrible to have brought this sad news with me," Hattie said. "It wasn't my intention at all, but when I learned about Christine being Lenore's daughter, well, I just thought it was the right thing to do." She frowned. "Unfortunately, I hadn't really thought about it being Christmas and all. It does seem like bad timing on my part. I hope Felicity can forgive me."

"You were right to tell us this, Hattie," Esther said. "Christmas or not, this wasn't a secret to keep hidden."

Jimmy was still shaking his head, but now tears were streaming down his cheeks. "I just can't—can't believe

170

that my dad would do something—something so—so horrible like that."

Esther nodded and then reached for his hand. "I know how you feel, Jimmy. This afternoon I was a complete crazy woman. Why, you should've seen me. I was breaking things and throwing things and—"

"Really?" Jimmy studied his stepmother more closely.

"It's true," Hattie said. "I only just finished cleaning it up, but the wreckage she left behind was something to behold."

"I feel like I'd like to break something too," Jimmy said in a flat voice.

"Be my guest," Esther said calmly. "Anything in here you'd like to take your hand to? Or maybe there's something left in the den that wasn't broken."

He sighed and looked down at his plate, one of the blue willow plates from her side of the family. Esther braced herself, afraid he was going to pick it up and throw it. And from where he was sitting and with his kind of arm, he could probably take out one of the French doors across from them. She prepared herself for a loud crash.

But he didn't throw it. "I know I have to forgive him," he finally said. "But at the moment, I just don't feel much like it. If he were here right now, I'd probably really let him have it. I feel like everything I ever believed about him has suddenly become a big, fat, ugly lie."

"If it helps," Hattie said in a gentle voice, "James was extremely sorry for what happened. Esther has all the letters he wrote to me during that time, shortly before he died . . . He confessed to everything in those letters, and he was very remorseful. Maybe you should read them too, Jimmy. It might help you understand better. Do you mind, Esther?"

"Not at all. I think it's a good idea. They're probably still on his desk."

Hattie left to go get them, and Jimmy leaned back in his chair. "I feel like somebody just knocked the wind out of me, Mom. Like I can't quite catch my breath."

"I know. Believe me, I know."

"Does Christine know about this yet?"

"Hattie told her."

"How did she take it?"

"She was understandably upset."

"Maybe that's why she left the house early today. Felicity was complaining about that tonight. She thought Christine was just being flaky."

"*Flaky* is not a word I would use to describe your half sister."

Jimmy's eyes opened wide. "You're absolutely right, Mom. Wow, I hadn't even thought of it like that. This *would* make her my half sister." He almost smiled. "Well, that's pretty cool."

Esther felt a small wave of relief.

"What's pretty cool?" Felicity snapped as she stepped back into the room, her eyes still red and swollen from crying.

"Christine is my half sister," Jimmy said with genuine enthusiasm. "I knew there was something familiar about that girl. She felt like family to me." Now he was grinning. "That means she's Jamie and Casey's aunt. Man, that's so cool."

"Oh, Jimmy!" Felicity sank back into her chair, folded

her arms across her chest, and scowled at him. "How do we even know this is true? I mean, Christine waltzes in here out of nowhere, and then she starts making all these claims and painting your dad out to be some sort of pervert who raped—"

"Felicity!" Esther felt her nostrils flare in anger, an unattractive habit she normally tried to avoid. "That is enough!" she said in her sternest voice. "You obviously don't have your facts straight about any of this."

"That's right, Felice," Jimmy said more gently. "Aunt Hattie has letters from Dad, confessing the whole thing to her."

"And here they are." Aunt Hattie set the bundle in front of Jimmy.

"Are you sure they're authentic?" Felicity asked in a small voice.

"Of course," Hattie said, slightly affronted. "Do you think I'd make something like this up about my own beloved brother? It was hard enough for me to know about this personally. Can you imagine how I struggled before I decided to tell the rest of you?"

"But the good news is that this makes Christine my half sister," Jimmy said. "And she's your niece, Aunt Hattie."

Hattie smiled. "Yes, I know. I'm so pleased."

"And my granddaughter," Esther said. "That is, if she hasn't given up on the bunch of us for jerking her around like this. Poor girl. She probably thinks she's suddenly landed in the loony family."

"Well, hopefully, we can make it up to her tomorrow," Hattie said.

"This will be her first Christmas with us," Jimmy said. "Our family is growing."

"So are we still on for the party?" Felicity asked in a tired voice. "Not that I really care so much anymore. Fact is, I wish I'd never agreed to this party in the first place. At the rate we're going, the whole thing will probably be a total disaster anyway."

"It's going to be okay, Felice," Jimmy reassured her.

"Yeah, right." She looked unconvinced. "Well, maybe we can stand around the Christmas tree and announce that the late great James Daniels was really a fraud who raped his stepdaughter."

"Felicity!" Jimmy's eyes narrowed, and Esther suspected that his wife had pushed it too far even for him this time. "That's totally uncalled for."

"Well, you people are so into making the truth known. Maybe everyone in town should know about this nasty little business. Maybe we should take out an ad—"

"Knock it off!" Jimmy stood. "I think we should go now. I'm sorry, Mom, Aunt Hattie. Felicity spoke way out of line just now."

"Don't apologize for me." Felicity stood up and reached for her coat slung over the back of her chair. "I'm not a child, you know."

"Then stop acting like one."

She looked at Jimmy as if he'd slapped her, and then she hurried from the room.

"Thanks for dinner," Jimmy said briskly. He jerked his arms into his jacket and shook his head. "Hopefully, Felicity and I can get this smoothed over before we ruin the holidays completely."

"Hopefully," Esther said without getting up.

"Good-night," Hattie said, ever cheerful. "Drive safely on the snow."

Esther exhaled loudly after the front door closed. "Well."

"Now, that didn't go too badly," Hattie said with a funny little grin.

Esther looked at her sister-in-law in wonder, and then they both laughed.

"I just hope Christine is all right," Esther said as she refolded her napkin and set it beside the plate.

"Well, I know I'll be saying a special prayer for that sweet little girl tonight."

Esther felt her brows lift slightly. "Really, Hattie? You've actually become a praying woman?"

She smiled. "Indeed, I have."

"Does this mean you believe in God and go to church and do all those churchy things that churchy people do?"

"I do believe in God, Esther, and I do go to church when I have a notion to. And I do pray and even read my Bible on occasion. But I wouldn't necessarily classify myself as a churchy person. I suppose it truly is hard to teach an old dog new tricks."

"So what on earth brought all this on?" Esther knew her voice sounded skeptical, perhaps even harsh, but she couldn't help herself. "I remember when you and Hal used to carouse and drink and gamble in Vegas with the best of them."

Hattie winked at her. "I figured at my age it was best to cover all my bets regarding the hereafter. I decided if God really was up there, and if he really did care about old Hattie, well, I thought it might be wise for old Hattie to give him a fair shot. And you know what, I think he does."

Esther considered this. "Very interesting, Hattie."

"You should give it some thought yourself, Esther. No offense, but you aren't getting any younger either."

"Thanks a lot."

Hattie's lips pressed together, and she grew quiet as if she were contemplating something. "There's another thing, Esther."

"Oh, no . . ." Esther held up her hands. "If it's more bad news about James, well, you better just sit on it for the time being. I'm not sure if I can handle anything else—"

"No, no, nothing like that. It's not anything bad. But you're right, it is about James. It's something he said to me on the phone about a week or so before he passed away."

Esther took in a quick breath, braced herself, and waited for Hattie to continue.

"At the time I wasn't too sure what to think. To be honest, I was still quite irked with him. Oh, I'd forgiven him all right, how could I not? But I secretly resented that he'd dumped this whole nasty business into my lap. It reminded me of when we were kids and he'd do something wrong and old Hattie would take the blame. But that evening when he called me, he told me that he'd made his peace with God. Now, I wasn't too sure what he meant by that. At that time in my life, I hadn't given God a second thought. But all these years later, I like to believe he meant that he'd received God's forgiveness. Although this is partial speculation on my part. But those were his words. He said,

'Don't worry about me, Hattie. I've made my peace with God.' And not long after that he died."

"Oh." Esther looked at the messy table before them and sighed. "Let's just leave this until tomorrow. I'm completely exhausted. I feel like I could sleep for a week."

"You and me both, Esther."

Esther imagined how the two of them must look as they slowly made their way through the semidarkened house. She, old and angular and clumsier than usual as she fumbled along on her crutches, and Hattie, short and round, taking her quick little steps alongside her. What a pair they made.

When Esther finally got herself into bed, she felt completely drained, but as she closed her eyes she thought of Christine and suddenly remembered what Hattie had said about praying for her tonight. Maybe it wouldn't hurt to give it a shot herself. At least she could do it for her granddaughter's sake, since she seemed to take this God thing pretty seriously.

"Well, God . . . ," she began slowly, "I know we're not really on much of a first name basis quite yet . . . I'm not even sure we'll ever be. But if you're up there listening, will you please watch out for my dear granddaughter tonight? Take care of her and bring her back to us safe and sound for Christmas. I'd really appreciate that. Amen."

19

Without bothering to remove her snow-dusted parka, Christine went straight for the phone in her dorm room. Her hands felt shaky as she attempted to dial the correct digits for the long-distance number to the mission station. Thankfully, she got it right the first time. She sighed in relief when a woman with an accent confirmed this on the other end. But when she asked for her father, she felt her heart drop to her snow-encrusted boots.

"I'm sorry," the woman said, "but Mr. Bradley has gone to spend the holidays with the Richards family. Their station is in the jungle, but we can reach your father by radio if it's an emergency."

"No, no . . ." Christine sighed. "It's not an emergency."

"Did you call to wish him a Merry Christmas?"

"Yes," Christine said sadly. "I'm sure he's having a wonderful time."

"Oh yes," the woman said. "Your father is a sweet man.

He was taking a lot of goodies out to share with the villagers. He's like a regular Saint Nick."

Despite herself, Christine smiled. "Yes, he is."

"God bless you," the woman said.

Christine hung up the phone and tried to imagine what it would be like to be down in Brazil, where summer was in full bloom right now. As much as she'd looked forward to a white Christmas, she would trade it in a heartbeat just to be down there in the heat and humidity with her dad.

"A regular Saint Nick," she said to herself. And even though it was the middle of the afternoon, she flopped down on her bed in total defeat. "So what would *you* do, Dad, if you were in my shoes right now?" The tears she'd been holding back began to fall freely. Not only for herself, although, to be honest, she was desperately homesick and lonely, more than she had ever been in her life. But mostly she felt sad for her mother—rather, her birth mother—Lenore. To think what that poor girl, a year younger than Christine, had endured during the last year of her life. So unfair and unjust. Christine could hardly even imagine it. It was so wrong!

"How could you let that happen to her, God?" she demanded. "And then to just let her die after all she'd been through? What was the purpose in all that?"

But no answers came, and before long the loneliness and emptiness of the vacated dormitory began to press against her, almost like a physical thing, breathing down her neck in short, chilly breaths. To remain in the isolation of that room for one more moment felt unendurable. So she pulled on her parka and gloves and headed over to her church. She hoped she might catch Pastor Reinhart and ask him some of these perplexing questions. He might not have all the answers, but at least he'd listen.

But when she arrived at the old brick church on Oak Street, she suddenly remembered that they'd opened their doors to offer shelter to the homeless during the holidays. Apparently, they did this every year at Christmastime. There was a homeless shelter downtown and a mission, but those ministries catered mostly to single adults. But the church went out of their way to create a special place where homeless families could gather and feel comfortable for a few days. Of course, Christine had been so distracted with her grandmother's family and all her related problems that she'd completely wiped it from her mind.

"Christine," Beth Maxwell called when Christine had barely reached the office. "What are you doing here?"

"Looking for Pastor Reinhart."

"He's in the kitchen at the moment."

"Thanks."

"Hey," Beth said hopefully, "before you skitter away, what are you doing the rest of the day?"

Christine shrugged. "Not much."

"Well, we're a little shorthanded," Beth said. Then she explained how she had broken the shelter kids into three age groups. "The teens are being treated to a free Christmas shopping spree at the local discount store, followed by a movie. And the middle graders are on their way to the skating rink, but the little kids were supposed to hang out here at the church for craft projects, snacks, and a special Christmas video."

"Sounds good."

"The problem is that Candace Everly was supposed to

be in charge of the little kids today, but her own kids just came down with the chicken pox, so she had to stay home. So we could really use your help, if you're willing."

"Sure," Christine said. Actually, she was happy to oblige. The last thing she wanted right now was to return to her ghost-town dorm and then sit around feeling sorry for herself. Instead she spent an amazingly stress-free afternoon with the youngest of the kids. Her biggest worry was whether or not they would run out of sequins and glitter as she helped their sticky little fingers cut and glue pieces of colored felt until they finally resembled Christmas stockings. She was surprised at how the time seemed to fly, and even after her responsibilities with the children were finished, Christine offered to stay on and help with dinner too.

"This is awfully nice of you, Christine," Pastor Reinhart said as she helped clean up afterward.

"Actually, it's kind of selfish," she admitted. "It helps keep my mind off of my own family troubles."

"You want to talk about it?" he asked.

But her problems suddenly seemed small in comparison with the problems of the families her church was trying to serve. She couldn't help but notice how poor they seemed, or how many of the parents' faces looked so apathetic or hopeless. She couldn't imagine how it would feel to be broke and homeless, especially during Christmas. And then to have children depending on them as well. It was so incredibly sad. But at least they had each other. That was something.

She felt reluctant to leave when Beth offered her a lift home. Of course, she knew it would be silly for her to take up one of the precious beds in the church's makeshift shelter, but it seemed almost preferable to returning to her empty dorm. In some ways she wasn't much more than homeless herself. Just the same, she accepted the ride and was thankful not to have to walk through what now appeared to be almost six inches of accumulated snow.

"Are you sure you want to stay by yourself at the dorm during Christmas?" Beth asked for the third time. She'd been incredulous that Christine had chosen to spend her holidays by herself at the dorm. "Really," she assured her. "You know you'd be welcome at my house."

"Thanks," Christine said. "But I'm fine, really. And I plan to come help out at the shelter again tomorrow, and then there's the candlelight service later on. Before I know it, Christmas will be over and done with and winter classes will be starting up again."

"Okay," Beth said. "Guess I'll see you tomorrow, then."

Christine trudged up the steps to her dorm, her tracks the only ones breaking into the most recent layer of snow. Of course, it made no sense to shovel the steps when the dorm was mostly empty. Plus, it was the holidays and the maintenance people were probably enjoying some time off. It also made little sense to run the big furnace at full blast, and a notice had been posted before winter break so that students would be prepared for the cooler temperatures. But it seemed to be getting colder and colder with each passing night.

Christine tried to imagine her dad in a steamy jungle setting, dressed as a jolly old elf and handing out gifts to the surprised indigenous locals and missionary kids. But suddenly all she could think of was poisonous spiders, gigantic snakes, and prowling panthers . . . and to her it seemed more perilous than ever for her sweet and unsuspecting father to be so far from home. She fervently prayed for his safety until she finally fell asleep.

20

Esther peered out the front window again. Long, blue shadows were falling across the snow, and the little white lights had come on and were starting to twinkle with false cheer. "Has anyone heard anything from Christine?" she asked.

"I've left two messages at her dorm," Jimmy said as he set a load of birch logs in the basket next to the fireplace. "Mind if I start this fire up now?"

"Go ahead," Felicity called from the dining room, where Esther had observed her arranging enough food to feed a small army. "We want it going nicely when the guests start to arrive."

"It's warm enough in here already," Esther snapped as she headed back toward her dining room to survey Felicity's latest damages. Felicity might be all gladness and joy today, and she'd even apologized for her thoughtless remarks last night, but Esther still felt certain that young woman was out to sabotage them all.

"Open a window if you're too warm," Felicity called in a voice as sweet as her heavily frosted Santa cookies.

It had grated on Esther's nerves all day—the way her daughter-in-law had waltzed in here as if everything was just fine. Oh, she'd done her little apology, with Jimmy at her elbow as if he'd personally coached her on the drive over. But Esther wasn't convinced. Now she hovered around Felicity, feeling a bit like a vulture on crutches. Scowling from her position in the doorway, she watched as Felicity flitted around the ornately decorated dining room table in her pretty red velvet party dress. *Queen for a day*, Esther thought as she turned in disgust, heading for the solitude of the den, what used to be James's den but was now her only haven in this normally quiet house that had suddenly turned into a three-ring circus. *Well, let them party if they must*, she thought as she closed the door behind her. Let stupid Felicity have her fun!

Oh, she knew she shouldn't take out her anger on poor Felicity. Why, that was like kicking the puppy who'd just chewed up your three-hundred-dollar shoes. What was the point? But Hattie had confessed to Esther during breakfast that morning that she felt fairly certain that Christine had overheard some of Felicity's thoughtless remarks the previous day. And now Esther felt certain that if Felicity had only possessed a little more sense and had treated Christine just a little better, well, maybe Christine would still be here with them today. And she'd told Jimmy as much that morning when he'd delivered the "special" load of firewood—special because it was birch and supposed to be "white and pretty." *Pretty, my foot*, she'd thought. *It's only firewood, for Pete's sake!*

185

"Christine is a sensible girl," Jimmy had reassured her. "I don't think she'd let something Felicity said upset her. Everyone knows that Felicity sometimes speaks without thinking."

"Sometimes?" Esther felt her left brow arch.

"Oh, Mom, Felicity may have her faults, but she's really not trying to hurt anyone intentionally. And, if it makes you feel any better, she was really very sorry by the time we got home last night. She almost called you, but it was getting pretty late by the time we got the kids to bed."

Be that as it may, Felicity had still done little besides the stilted apology to convince Esther of her contrition. And Esther felt seriously fed up with her daughter-in-law as she sank down into the big leather chair behind James's old desk. She leaned back and looked around her. Hattie had done a good job of cleaning up. And the den actually looked much better with all of James's ridiculous paraphernalia removed. Much more calming and peaceful. She should've done it years ago.

Esther looked at the black desk phone and even picked up the receiver. But then she'd already called that number several times and left at least two, maybe three, messages. Still, she supposed it wouldn't hurt to try again. But she was answered by the same old thing; after four rings the blasted machine came on again.

"You've reached the number of Christine Bradley and Brianna Taylor. Please—" Esther put the receiver back in the cradle with a thud. *Where could that girl be?* As far as Esther knew she didn't have any relatives nearby and all her friends had gone home for the holidays. Perhaps she'd called one of them up, desperate to escape the insanity of the Daniels family, and begged to be included in some festivity. Maybe she was off at some ski lodge, having a good time with friends and drinking hot toddies right now. That's what Esther would've been doing at the same age. Goodness, how many times had she opted for some expensive and scintillating outing with friends over going home to spend time with family? And did she regret it now? Well, of course she did. But not completely.

"Oh, who can figure such things out?" she said to herself. She felt exasperated and agitated and suddenly longed for a cigarette like she hadn't done in years. Oh, she knew it was perfectly ridiculous and would probably make her sick, but she simply felt the need for something to calm her nerves. She began jerking open the drawers to James's desk. Surely, he must've left something behind, since he'd smoked right up to the day he died. Naturally, the drawers were full of all sorts of odd things, and she wished she'd taken the time to dump their contents onto the floor yesterday. Perhaps Hattie would've gotten rid of all that junk too. Not that she wished to turn Hattie into her personal maid. Actually, she was becoming rather fond of her previously estranged sister-in-law. But right now Hattie was having a little nap, refreshing herself before the guests started to arrive, and all Esther wanted was a stupid cigarette!

Of course, Esther knew she might've been wise to have followed Hattie's lead and taken a nap. After all, she had every reason to excuse herself from all of Felicity's hubbub. She could've said, "I'm so sorry, but I'm recovering from a bad sprain and really need my rest." She'd be sorry once the party really got going. The extra people in her home had begun to wear her already frazzled nerves thin.

Good-night, why couldn't she find any darn cigarettes?

"Voila!" she said triumphantly when she finally unearthed a sleek silver case with the initials JD on it. She'd gotten him this for their fifteenth anniversary, shortly before he became ill and was told to give up smoking, which he did not.

The case felt light, and she expected it to be empty as she popped it open, but there, as if appointed by fate, lay one lonely cigarette.

"Ahhh." She picked it up and smelled the pungent, earthy smell of stale tobacco. Then she put it to her lips before she looked around and realized she needed a light. After more digging and hunting, she finally discovered a dusty old book of matches. She blew off the dust and examined the faded photo on the front. Something about that large pink building and palm trees seemed vaguely familiar. Without her reading glasses, she was forced to hold it at arm's length, squinting to read the fine print. *The Hotel Marquise*. Ah, yes, it was where she and James had stayed during their honeymoon in the Bahamas—about twenty-three years ago now. She set the cigarette and matchbook on the surface of the desk, then pulled back her hand as if these items were hot coals. Then, as if mesmerized, she just stared at them.

Is this what life eventually boils down to? A stale cigarette and a dusty book of matches? Two seemingly innocent items that burn you clear to your soul? She pushed herself up from the chair and limped painfully over to the leather sofa. She fell down onto it in a broken heap, clutched a tapestry-covered cushion, and began to sob. "I am nothing but a useless old woman," she moaned. "I have led a foolish and shallow life with nothing to show for it but ashes and dust . . . ashes and dust. Nothing left . . . but ashes and dust."

21

Christine had managed to maintain a brave front for the whole day as she poured all her energy into the homeless shelter. But by that evening, she felt worn and weary, and just slightly beaten. It wasn't the work so much, although she couldn't remember having labored so long or so hard in her life. Being young and healthy, she'd stepped up and volunteered for the hardest task of all, kitchen crew. And not just for a one-meal shift or cleanup or setup; no, she'd stuck her foot in her mouth and volunteered to help out with everything for the entire day. And, naturally, they were happy to have her.

Still, it wasn't the work that had eventually worn her down, but rather her surrounding circumstances. Seeing and interacting with all those homeless families, those children who seemed hungry for not only food but also the slightest speck of attention, those young single mothers with worn-out shoes and empty eyes.

Well, it had finally managed to wear her down, and

now that the day was over, her cheeks were tired from smiling and she felt seriously depressed. But perhaps the most shameful part of all this was that she wasn't just depressed over their sad lots in life and how they had nothing, no homes, no money, no means. No, that might actually seem noble or admirable, expected even.

If the truth were told, and she hoped it never would be, Christine was feeling sorry for herself because at least those poor homeless people had fragments of their families around them during Christmas, whereas she felt entirely cut off and alone. And to realize that she was actually feeling jealous of homeless families—now, really, how pathetic was that?

If she hadn't been so tired, so thoroughly down and out, she might've found her situation to be somewhat humorous. She might've imagined herself talking to her dad on the phone after the New Year and telling him the whole embarrassing story, and then they would both laugh and he would promise that they would have a grand Christmas after he came home in two years, or better yet, maybe they could figure out a way to fly her down there for Christmas next year.

But as she slipped into the back pew of the packed church, she felt no joy, no mirth, no Christmas cheer. In fact, she wondered why she'd even bothered to come to the candlelight service at all. Chances were it would only depress her more as she saw families clustered together, sharing candles and smiles and warm embraces. The old man beside her smiled and nodded, then turned his attention back to the pulpit. She didn't recognize him, but she'd been attending this church only a few months and hadn't had a chance to meet everyone.

She tried to pay attention as Pastor Reinhart spoke of the first Christmas, but she found herself drifting in and out. Of course, she'd heard the Christmas message so many times that she knew it by heart. Maybe she was just tired. Maybe she should just go home before she nodded off to sleep and really embarrassed herself.

She stood up and slipped unnoticed out the back of the church and then out the door to the street. But before she turned to walk back to her dorm, she paused to look at the nativity scene that was set up in front of the church. Oh, she'd seen it before and had even admired the painted life-size plywood figures of Mary and Joseph, the shepherds and angels and animals, all propped up beneath the straw-covered roof of a "stable." And they almost looked real in the soft spotlights tonight. Christine studied Mary and the way her sad eyes seemed to gaze fondly at the baby in the manger. Mary had been even younger than Christine when she'd been chosen to bear God's child. A teen mother. *Not so unlike Lenore*, Christine thought. It couldn't have been easy for either of them. Surely, Mary must've had times when she wondered what God was up to. It would've been a challenge to be the mother of God's son, and although she was called "blessed," she certainly must've suffered some too.

Christine knew that Lenore had suffered dearly for the baby she carried as well. To be only eighteen and to stand against her parents, fighting to protect her baby's life—Christine's life. She shuddered. Not so different from Mary in some ways.

Christine pulled on her gloves and began walking toward her dorm. But as she walked she considered her birth mother's life and how it was similar to Mary's. Surely, God's hand had been on Lenore during those hard times. How else would she have been befriended by Christine's loving parents? Oh, Christine knew that God hadn't willed for Lenore to be raped. No, that was just one of those unfortunate circumstances where sin got in the way. But, ultimately, according to Christine's father, Lenore had been happy to give birth, and she'd been pleased and proud of her baby daughter. And although it wasn't easy to give her up, Lenore had entrusted Christine to this kind and generous couple. And Christine's parents had been overjoyed at Lenore's incredible gift of love.

Christine stopped on a corner and looked up at the dark sky. "Thank you, God," she whispered, finally believing that perhaps her life wasn't a mistake after all, that perhaps God was still in control, that he still loved her and wanted the best for her.

She continued to walk, still thinking about young Lenore and her brave decision to keep her baby despite the circumstances. Christine wasn't sure she would be as brave under similar conditions. Suddenly she was flooded with gratitude and respect for her birth mother. Suddenly she wished there was a way she could tell her. She stopped again. "Please, God," she whispered to the night. "Please, tell my mother Lenore I want to say thank you to her too." Christine realized it was probably a foolish prayer, but she meant it with her whole heart. She stood there for a long moment, just silently staring into the almost-black sky, when suddenly she noticed a star breaking through the clouds, as if it was peering down at her, as if it was winking. Oh, she knew it was silly and probably her imagination, but it seemed like a sign. As if Lenore was trying to reassure her that all was well in heaven. "Thank you," Christine breathed.

And then she saw another star, just as bright as the first, popping out right next to the other one. The only two stars she could see in the entire night sky. Suddenly Christine laughed as she imagined her two mothers holding hands in heaven. "And tell my mother Marie I said thank you too," she whispered. She stood there just staring at the pair of twinkling stars, and then suddenly she saw a third star, directly across from the other two, making a perfect triangle. "And, while you're at it, please tell Jesus's mother Mary I said thank you too."

Then, with a lighter heart than she'd had in weeks, Christine walked back to the dorm. She knew that not everything was resolved, and she knew she still had to figure out what her role would be with the Daniels family. But she also knew that things had changed between her and Lenore. She knew that she'd be forever grateful for her birth mother, forever thankful that she'd saved Christine's life. And she owed it to Lenore to do whatever she could for her surviving family.

Christine had barely closed the door to her room before she saw the message light flashing on her answering machine. Hoping it was her dad, she turned it on. "You have seven messages," the electronic voice said. Surprised at the number, she played them all to discover that none were from her dad. But she was relieved, since the only reason she'd hear from him right now would probably be due to an emergency. Besides, three of the messages were from her grandmother, all urging her to come over to the house, to bring her things, and to stay until New Year's. And one message was from Aunt Hattie, saying how much she missed her little niece and to please come back by the house before she had to return home. And two were from Jimmy, saying that he was so happy to learn that she was his half sister and would she please give them a call as soon as she got in. And one was actually from Felicity, an apology of sorts, saying that she hoped Christine hadn't misunderstood her, but that that sometimes happened, and how much the children would love to see her for Christmas.

"Well." Christine picked up the phone and quickly dialed. She waited through several rings until she heard Jimmy's voice over what sounded like a houseful of others.

"Christine!" he boomed. "Merry Christmas! Are you coming over?"

"I could," she began. "If it's not too late."

"Never too late for you. Are you at your dorm right now? How about I pop over and pick you up? I don't like the idea of my little sister walking by herself at night."

So it was settled. Christine hurried to change her clothes. No sense showing up in her soiled kitchen clothes that smelled like green beans and turkey gravy. Then she grabbed the photo album she'd assembled for Grandmother. She wished she'd taken time to do something for the others. Oh well, maybe next year.

Jimmy cheerfully filled her in on all the happenings of the day and the party as they drove. "A lot of Felicity's family and friends are there. And as you can imagine, Mom's been lying low for most of the evening. I think she's been worried about you." He parked the car in the spot still left in the driveway. But the side streets were filled with cars.

"I'm sorry," Christine said. "I've been helping at my church, but I should've called."

"Hey, I don't blame you," he said as they reached the front door. Then suddenly he hugged her. "And just so you know, I'm really glad that you're my sister, Christine. Welcome to the family. Really." Then they walked inside, and he took her coat and nudged her down the hallway. "Your grandmother is in the den," he whispered.

Before anyone noticed her arrival, Christine slipped off to find her. She tapped lightly on the den door, but due to the noise from the party—a boisterous group was attempting to sing "The Twelve Days of Christmas" around the piano—she decided to simply let herself in. And there, sitting behind the big mahogany desk, was her grandmother, head bent down as she held a match in a somewhat shaky hand to light a rather bent cigarette.

"Grandmother?"

She looked up at Christine, her face an odd mixture of simultaneous embarrassment and pleasure. "Oh! You're here," she sputtered through the smoke.

"Yeah." Christine smiled. "Merry Christmas, Grandmother."

She sheepishly held out the cigarette. "I thought I needed this, but . . ."

"Don't let me stop you," Christine said as she sat down in the chair across from the desk, placing the photo album in her lap.

"Do you think smoking is a sin?" her grandmother

196

asked, still holding the cigarette at a distance as if she wasn't quite sure what to do with it.

"I think God's the only one who can determine that," Christine said with a smile.

"Really?" Esther looked at her cigarette with curiosity, then took a tentative puff followed by a short fit of coughing. "Hand me that ashtray, will you?"

Christine reached for the brass dish on the coffee table and set it on the desk, watching as her grandmother snuffed the cigarette out and sighed.

"It was just for old times' sake," Grandmother said, still sputtering. "But I guess my lungs weren't ready for it."

"I have something for you," Christine said. "For old times' sake."

"Really?" Grandmother leaned forward with interest, and Christine slid the photo album across the smooth surface of the desk.

"Sorry, I didn't have time to wrap it."

Esther slowly opened the album, then just stared at the array of photos before her. It was only the first page, and only shots of Christine as a newborn, a rather red and wrinkly looking baby. After what seemed several minutes her grandmother turned to the next page, staring again with equal fascination.

Christine leaned over the desk to see the album more clearly. She wondered if there was something more fascinating than she'd realized. "That was my first birthday," Christine said, pointing to the redheaded infant dressed like an elf in green velvet.

Esther nodded without speaking, and Christine wondered if perhaps this wasn't such a good idea after all. But she sat, waiting patiently while her grandmother slowly worked her way through the book. The last pictures had been taken at Christine's high school graduation, and then there was one of her and her father shortly before he left for Brazil.

"Thank you," Esther said in a low voice.

"I hope it's okay."

Her grandmother looked at her. "Are you kidding? Okay? Why, it's one of the most beautiful gifts I've ever received. Thank you." She flipped back through it again, staring in wonder at the photos, then suddenly looked up. "So you must have a December birthday too."

Christine nodded.

"What day is it?"

Christine never liked to answer this question, but she finally said, "The twenty-fifth."

"Christmas day?"

She nodded. "Yeah. My parents called me their Christmas present."

Her grandmother smiled. "I can understand that." She looked back down at the book. "Now, can you tell me more about what's going on in these pictures?" she asked. "Like where were you when this was taken?"

So for the next hour or so, Christine attempted to commentate on the pictorial tour of her life.

"Hello in there," Jimmy called as he poked his head in the door. "Everything okay?"

"Yes, of course," Esther said. "How's the party going?"

"Nearly everyone has gone home now, except for immediate family."

"Is it that late?" Esther looked at her watch. "Good heavens, it's half past eleven."

"You two care to join us for a cup of peppermint cocoa?"

"Yes," Esther said. "In fact, I have a little announcement to make."

22

After everyone had gathered comfortably in the living room, where a cheerful fire was still snapping in the fireplace, Jimmy brought out a tray of cocoa cups, each one topped with a dollop of whipping cream and garnished with a candy cane.

"Remember who started this tradition?" Jimmy asked as he handed Grandmother a steaming cup.

"Haven't we always done this?" Felicity said as she picked up a cup for herself.

"Well, I never did it myself," Jimmy said as he handed Christine a cup. "Not until Dad married Mom, that is." He handed Aunt Hattie a cup. "But I believe it was Lenore's tradition to have cocoa before bed on Christmas Eve."

"To give you sweet dreams," Grandmother said in a voice full of reflection.

Jimmy sat down next to his wife. "Works for me."

"Too late for them," Aunt Hattie said as she nodded to

Jamie and Casey, who were curled up in sleeping bags beneath the Christmas tree.

"It was Jamie's idea to bring the sleeping bags," Jimmy said. "But don't worry, Mom, they don't need to spend the night here."

She waved her hand. "Oh, that's all right, they're welcome to stay if they like."

Jimmy blinked, then Felicity spoke quickly. "No, we have to go over to my mom's in the morning. She's making waffles."

"Good for you," Grandmother said. "Good for Janet." She looked around the room, pausing to look at each face before she continued to speak. "As I told you, I have a little announcement to make tonight. But I didn't want to make it until everyone was here." She looked directly at Christine. "My family isn't very big, but you're all important to me. As you know, I've been in contact with my lawyer regarding my will. He made a draft today, and I will sign it after the holidays." She chuckled. "And be assured, if I should kick the bucket between now and then, the changes I made today will be in effect."

Christine glanced over at Jimmy and Felicity. She could tell by Felicity's creased brow that she was worried. And Christine knew that all this talk about changing the will had been upsetting to her. Suddenly Christine wished that she could just disappear. She had no idea what her grandmother was up to, but she was worried that her own presence had been the catalyst behind it.

"Rather than wait for my timely or untimely demise, I've decided to make my wishes known while I'm still around to make sure no bickering occurs after I'm gone."

She turned and looked directly at Felicity. "Because despite what I've said about money all these years, I know as well as anyone that it will never buy you happiness. Just the same, I know that's a whole lot easier to say when money's not an issue." She cleared her throat, then glanced over at Aunt Hattie. "Sorry you have to hear all this again, Hattie."

"That's perfectly all right, dear. You go right ahead."

"So what I have decided to do is to disburse some of your inheritance now," Grandmother said. "Not all of it, mind you. Some things are better left until the end. But I have decided that it makes no sense for an old woman like me to sit on a pile of money while some folks are struggling to make ends meet."

"Oh, Mom," Jimmy began. "You don't need to—"

"You just hush now, Jimmy. You're a good boy, and I love you like my own, but when it comes to money sense you don't always get it." She shook her finger at him, then smiled. "Anyway, as I was saying . . . I want everything to be perfectly clear. I know how easy it is to get confused when families and wealth merge in marriages. I want all my cards laid out on the table. You see, when Christine's mother left home more than twenty years ago, she had a good-size savings account that her father had started for her for college when she was just an infant. This was an account that I continued to add to over the years, hoping that someday she would come home and I would—" She choked slightly, and Aunt Hattie patted her hand.

"Anyway, at first I just wanted to change my will to reflect that this savings is to go to Christine. Because that seems only fair. But that's when I decided that it's usually the very times when kids need money that they don't have it. And that's when I decided to do a little disbursing this Christmas." She held out two envelopes. One she pointed in Christine's direction, the other in Jimmy's. "Well, come on, here you go. Merry Christmas."

Jimmy got up and got his envelope, but Christine felt like she couldn't move. Then Jimmy got hers and handed it to her. "Come on, Christine, don't be upsetting your grandma on Christmas Eve."

"That's right," said Grandmother. "And like I said, that's your inheritance for now. I plan to keep my house and enough to live comfortably on for . . . well, at least until I see those grandchildren grow up." She looked at Christine. "And perhaps see some great-grandchildren from you. In due time, that is. No hurry."

Christine felt her cheeks blushing. Then without looking inside the envelope, she got up and went over to hug her grandmother. "Thanks," she whispered.

"Thank *you*," Grandmother said.

When Christine stepped back she could see her grandmother's blue eyes glistening with tears, but for a change they seemed like tears of joy.

Just then the bell on the mantle clock began to ring.

"Look, everyone, it's midnight now," Jimmy said. "Merry Christmas, everyone!"

"Happy birthday, Christine," Grandmother said.

"No way," said Jimmy. "You're a Christmas baby?"

She nodded with embarrassment.

"Happy birthday, dear," Aunt Hattie said with a smile.

"Happy birthday," Felicity said. "Just wait'll Jamie hears

about this. He thought it was bad being born the week before Christmas."

Christine nodded. "Yeah, it always made having parties a little awkward. But it was kind of fun too."

"Her parents called her their Christmas present," Grandmother said with a bright smile.

"That makes me think of something," Aunt Hattie said as she held up her cocoa cup. "I'd like to propose a Christmas toast."

Everyone else held up their cups and waited.

"Here's to Christmas Past," began Aunt Hattie. "The gift we keep with us forever. And here's to Christmas Future." She glanced at the children peacefully snoozing beneath the Christmas tree. "The gift that is yet to come. And here's to Christmas Present." Aunt Hattie nodded to Christine and smiled. "The gift we open today!"

Melody Carlson is the prolific author of more than seventy books of fiction, nonfiction, and gift books for adults, young adults, and children. Her most recent novels are *Amanda's Treasure* (Tyndale, 2004) and *Finding Alice* (Water Brook, 2003). Her writing has won several awards, including a Gold Medallion for *King of the Stable* (Crossway, 1998) and a Romance Writers of America Rita award for *Homeward* (Multnomah, 1997). She lives with her husband in central Oregon.